THE VAMPIRE'S CITY

MARY E. TWOMEY

MARY E. TWOMEY, LLC

THE VAMPIRE'S CITY

Book One in The Last Deadblood Series

By

Mary E. Twomey

COPYRIGHT

Copyright © 2021 Mary E. Twomey LLC
Cover Art by Emcat Designs

All rights reserved.
First Edition: September 2021

For information:
http://www.maryetwomey.com

DEDICATION

To the younger, more optimistic me.

I know you're still in there somewhere.

ABOUT THE VAMPIRE'S CITY

When Colette returns to her hometown after a decade away, she knows her life will never be the same.

With the war between the two families finally cooling, Colette returns to Mayfield determined to improve relations in the divided city the only way she knows how. Opening up a business that serves both humans and vampires isn't going to win her any friends, but she didn't expect enemies to pop up so quickly.

Danger lurks in the shadows as she does all she can to repair the broken city she left behind so many years ago. Now with her head held high and her father's stubborn nature in her veins, Colette collides with the one vampire whom she knows could shatter her plans—and her heart.

"The Vampire's City" is filled with political intrigue and scandalous secrets, written by USA Today bestselling fantasy romance author, Mary E. Twomey.

1

RISKY BUSINESS MOVE
COLETTE

This is a safe area, I remind myself. No vampire attacks have been deadly in at least six months, and no humans have assaulted a vampire in as much time, either. We're a peaceful town now.

Or at least, that's what they brag they are.

Yet when the backdoor of my shop swings open and I hear an unfamiliar tread coming toward me, I clutch the broom in my fists, ready to weaponize the thing if need be.

I'm not scared.

I've told myself as much every hour all day. One of these times it will ring true.

My gaze snags on the three spots around the salon where I've hidden guns, just in case.

A shotgun behind the picture of a voluptuous hair model hanging on the wall.

A Colt 1911 in my office.

A Glock 9mm behind the cash register in the hostess stand, which has been painted the color "Angel's Kiss". That is another word for pearly white, I have learned. The entire design is in line with my brand, but as this is only my third branch I have ever opened, I still feel the pangs of worrying I am too green for this sort of leap.

Especially considering that this branch is in Midtown in the wary metropolitan area of Mayfield. I am the last person whom this city wants to see opening a business in these parts. Being me has caused enough trouble for this town.

Yet here I am, because I have a plan.

A really stupid plan to bring unity to a city that is completely divided.

I am determined to do this by myself, with nothing but a few gutsy stylists and three guns.

And I am going to do it barefoot, apparently, since I left my heels in my office because my feet were killing me.

I take a deep breath and do what I can to remain calm.

I belong where I put myself, and I have set down roots here, for better or worse.

A male voice jerks my heart around in my chest as a man I once knew well walks in from the back exit.

"Well, would you look at that," he says about the broom in my hand. "Apparently the Kennedy family *can* clean up its messes. Who knew?"

Nico Valentino strolls in, his shoulders back to feign ease, as if it's totally fine that he just picked the lock and broke into my business unannounced.

My breath catches at both the intrusion and the intruder. Seeing the youngest Valentino brother for the first time after so many years spent apart drives a knife through my chest. Everything in me aches at the sight of Nico, though I know the attachment is entirely one-sided, now that we play by the rules the grownups have set out for us.

My childhood best friend is all grown up, as am I. Yet here we are, divided for reasons that had nothing to do with us.

The instinct to run into his arms is overwhelming, though I know that is not who we are to each other anymore.

When I chose to open a business in Midtown—the only Kennedy to ever attempt something so bold (or stupid)—I knew there would be risks.

Still, I pretend I am not the least bit affected by the impromptu visitor. I make sure to keep my voice light. "If you stopped by for a haircut, I don't open my doors until Monday."

Both the Valentino brothers have that cocky way to them. Though I haven't seen Nico in years, other than watching him get arrested and then worm his way out of jail on TV, he still looks the exact same—lean build, thin lips, and a medium height that is somehow still forbidding in nature. His jet-black hair is coupled with olive skin that only tans, never burns. He's got the thick, expressive eyebrows of all the men in that family. His angular jaw adds a touch of cruelty to his infrequent smiles.

Of course, I remember back when he was Nino-bear, and we made mud pies together.

But that was before our fathers made a mess of things.

Nico throws the sign I had hanging on the front of my door. *Vampires and Humans Welcome* is a big statement, but it shouldn't be. It should be a given that everyone is welcome in every business. Of course, nearly every other business in Midtown hangs signs that read *Humans Only*.

I opened my business here to make a statement, to make peace, to force the world to make sense.

Nico runs a hand across the closely shaven sides of his head. "You gonna make me all pretty, Deadblood?"

I've always hated that nickname. Though, I'm not sure it qualifies as a nickname. Those are supposed to be playful and cute, not a moniker to make me sound infamous for being born the way I was.

My smile is breezy but my grip on the broom is tight, my knuckles paling as the seconds tick by. "Only the best for you. Maybe some highlights, a waxing between your eyebrows—you know, so there's two of them."

Nico mimes a laugh and claps his hands. "I was

thinking you might want to postpone your grand opening. Put it off a few months."

Though he is taller than me even if I was wearing my heels, the fact that I am barefoot makes me feel like he outgrew me by a mile. Nico is dressed like he knows how to get rid of a body, what with the standard black slacks and white button-down every man in or working for the Valentino family wears like it's a uniform. My pink pencil skirt and cream blouse that show off my curves made me feel pretty, feminine and powerful when I put them on this morning, but now I wish I'd opted for combat boots and Kevlar.

I fight to keep my voice steady, but it comes out a mild squeak. "What are you doing here, Nico?"

I can handle the press without breaking a noticeable sweat. I can give the reporters their pictures without an ounce of hesitation in my smile nor a brunette curl out of place. I can hold my head up as if being the Last Deadblood is no strain on my soul.

But being in the same room as my childhood best friend (who now hates my very existence) requires constant effort to keep my composure from crumbling.

Nico rolls up the sleeves of his white dress shirt. "I'm helping you get ready. You look like you could use a hand."

I shouldn't be surprised when he grabs up the nearest chair and bashes it against the long mirror I installed yesterday beside the entrance.

I tense at the shatter of glass that litters the floor, but I keep my scream to myself.

I expected hazing from the vampires who are certain I shouldn't exist. I am the Last Deadblood, after all.

Nico's roar of frustration rattles my insides. "You think you can come back to Mayfield and we're just going to let you? It's bad enough that you didn't stay gone, but to open up a business here, smack in the center of Midtown?" He motions around the salon that I have made sure is nearly perfect. "Maybe if you'd stayed in the East End with the other humans, I wouldn't have to come here and lay down a few ground rules. But opening a business where vampires have to look at you and deal with all you've done is a new low, even for you Kennedys."

I don't argue. There's no point. I have been responsible for the deaths of hundreds of vampires, however indirectly.

To make matters worse, my father could have used his office as sheriff to go after the criminals who murdered vampires. They made weapons using my blood, which is a surefire way to kill a vampire. But for a good many years, my father turned a blind eye to the plight of those not like him.

My father is supposed to protect *all* the citizens of Mayfield, instead of just the ones who are most like him.

It set a precedent to the rest of the world that vampires are second-class citizens, undeserving of justice.

Father has come to his senses and cracked down harder on violence against vampires since then, but the stink of his lax rule isn't something the vampires are quick to forgive, nor humans reticent to exploit.

Clearly Nico will never be ready to forgive my family's sins.

Never mind that I was sent away during the major clashes between my family and Nico's. Forget that I have been the one campaigning for peace every time I am interviewed. Forget that for the vampires to be in danger from the radicals because of me, *I* have to be in danger by the radicals, as well. In no way would I ever donate my deadly blood to people intent on murdering vampires.

Nature is cruel, but people are worse.

All anyone sees when they look at me is a Deadblood, no matter how much I try to convince the world I want these stupid turf wars to end.

I try to keep my voice level. "Nico, enough. I have every right to be here. I belong where I put myself."

"You belong anywhere other than Mayfield." Nico sets the chair down, whistling a menacing tune. Actually, it's a light, whimsical ditty, but on his curved, slender lips, the tune turns sinister and sends a chill up my spine. "If you get to be a hairstylist, then I get to be a decorator. That window looks a little off to me."

I wince when he takes the chair and bashes it against the giant picture window.

Fear rockets through me when I realize that coming home might be the worst mistake I will ever make.

And Nico will never tire of making me pay for it.

2

OLD GRUDGES
COLETTE

The chair bounces off the surface without leaving a scratch, though Nico's rage is still in full swing.

I examine my nails, feigning boredom, even though I am shaking inside. "Bulletproof glass. I had it installed to make sure any of your kind that come in here are safe."

"My kind?" Nico snarls at me, launching the chair across the salon. "You can say it, Colette. I'm a vampire. And the only bullets that could take us out are the ones coated with your blood. If you really wanted to protect us, you would stay away from Mayfield. You wouldn't have been used to make all those weapons designed to slaughter *my kind*."

I swallow hard, unable to pretend Nino-bear's accusations don't wound me.

That's who he was to me, back when we were too

young to care that we shouldn't be friends. He was my Nino-bear, and I was his Coco-bear.

I straighten, still holding my broom as if it's a shield. "You know I had nothing to do with that. I would never hurt you on purpose."

Nico spits on the floor I just finished sweeping. "That stupid treaty isn't worth the paper it's printed on. It's got your father's signature on it, and he's never been anything but a liar."

I'll not argue with that.

I smooth out my blouse, refusing to look ruffled. I don't want Nico to know how upset him being here makes me. In my silly imagination, I've envisioned the first time I come across my childhood best friend, all grown up. How it plays out in my mind is that we accidentally run into each other on the street in Midtown. Worry twists my features because I don't want him to hate me, or worse, not remember my face. But he breaks through my anxiety with a pure smile, scooping me in a hug while he excitedly catches me up on the adventures I've missed in his life's journey while I was overseas.

I comment on how grown he looks, and he spouts back a comment about me not growing at all, because I'm still so short. We share a laugh and then we go to a coffee shop to spend the afternoon together and catch up. We marvel over how crazy the world is, and how we are the only two sane ones left.

Not quite the scene playing out before me now.

I am prepared for this, even though it breaks my heart. My best plan is to pretend I don't have a heart, that the useless organ holds no value.

I lift my chin. "My father is who he is, but I am who I am. I've never killed a single person unless it was self-defense or by accident."

Nico scoffs. "But your blood was used to coat the bullets that killed my people."

And here it comes. I can feel the years of resentment bubbling up, now that I am back in town and Nico has somewhere to spew his pent-up venom.

He is one of thousands who have every right to hate me for all my blood has done. I'll not rob him of his fury. Now that I am back in Mayfield after so many years away, I'm sure this will be the first of many interactions wherein I absorb the brunt of their well-earned hatred brought on by the world's injustice and my cursed genetics.

Nico's cheeks turn red with rage. "Your bullets killed my mom!"

Though his words are true, and I've done my best to deal with them over the past four years, they shove me in the chest all the same. Images of the only mom I have ever known flood my brain. Even though she was never rightfully mine, I claimed her as such, and she smiled every time.

The fact that my blood was used to murder Mama V is

a crime I will never forgive the world for, nor will I forgive myself.

"I loved her, too," I offer, though I know this is the wrong thing to say.

Nico picks up another chair and starts wailing at the drywall, carving huge holes into the freshly painted lavender surface.

I grimace, anxiety climbing in my veins. I want to race to stop him, but I know that would only make things worse.

Nico beats on the wall. "Fat lot of good your love did her! If not for you and your family, she would still be alive!"

I back up until my spine hits the far wall, bracing myself as Nico destroys much of my hard work. My fingers itch to grab my Glock 9mm from the register, but reason wins out.

Though mine are just regular bullets that can't kill a vampire, they send a clear enough message. They can slow a vampire down, even going so far as cracking bone. But though the temptation is there, I am not going to hurt Nico, no matter how much of a prick he's turned out to be.

I'm not sure I am capable of raising my hand to a Valentino.

My blood murdered Nico's mother. Maybe this is a portion of what I owe him.

Nico knows I wanted peace between the families, so he

is banking on the belief that I won't hurt him, even when he is determined to destroy the one thing I came back to Mayfield to do.

I didn't think restoring peace to my hometown would be as easy as opening up a salon that caters to both humans and vampires in Midtown, but it's a start.

And Nino-bear is currently destroying my progress.

"I did love her," I say again, knowing I should just shut up. Memories of Mama Valentino braiding my brown hair in fancy styles when I was a little girl flood my brain.

Red lipstick. Always red. Black hair smooth as silk. No matter how often I try to scrub my mind of Mama V's sweetness, I can still see it, even as her son trashes my business.

"It was your blood that killed her." The finger Nico jabs in my direction feels like a knife to my chest. I recognize it because I stab myself with it often enough. "If not for you, she would still be alive. Dad hated you until his dying day for getting his wife murdered."

Bile rises in my throat. Any chance at remaining in control of my faculties is compromised as self-loathing washes over me, dousing me from head to toe. "No," I whisper, though I know Nico isn't lying. He is many things —mainly insane—but he's not a liar. Liars are a Valentino's worst enemy.

Which explains why they have been at odds with my father and oldest brother for so long.

I try to reason with Nico, clearly having lost my hold on rationality. "I was tied up when those criminals took my blood. I tried to escape, but I couldn't!"

Nico drops the stool so he can grip the two inches of black hair on top of his head, pulling on the strands as if I have driven him to this madness on purpose. "I don't want to hear how *you're* the victim in my mother's murder!"

His words smack me across the face, building the pressure behind my eyes. "I loved your mother! She was the only mom I ever had!"

Another hole in the wall, though Nico still is not satisfied. "Yeah? Well, if your mother was still alive, I would have tracked her down and put a bullet through her head, so you would know how this feels. And now you're opening up a business in Midtown? Now I have to see your face in this part of town? Do you know how few places vampires have that are relatively safe?"

Moisture pricks my eyes, but emotion will do me no good here. The only thing that could stop this are the guns that are calling out to me from their hidden places.

No. I will not become who they tell me I am. I won't be the mass-murderer fate designed me to be.

But I also won't be the one taking the blame for every bit of violence that painted our city red for all those years.

I didn't know. I was a kid when our family doctor took my blood every week. She'd told me I was sick, and she needed to check my blood often to be sure I was healthy.

She was my mother's physician too, before my mother died.

I didn't know the doctor was absconding with the high concentration of venom meant to kill vampires that produces naturally in women in my family's blood. It remains dormant in the men but runs rampant in the females of the Kennedy family tree.

I didn't know about any of it. I was all about making my red popsicle dye my lips so I could pretend I was wearing lipstick, like Mama Valentino.

Angst riddles my voice when I dare speak up for myself. "My father took my brothers and me to your house every week, Nico. Do you think any of us knew what my doctor was up to? I wasn't eating popsicles in the backyard with you while secretly plotting a murder spree when I was five years old."

"I don't want to hear it!" Nico discards the chair and starts in on the welcome desk. There's no cash in the register yet, but the cost of the damage is adding up by the second. Judging by the way he's battering the thing with the stool, it won't be fit to hold a single coin.

I have invested more than one hundred thousand dollars of my own to open this place. And now even more will be required to repair the damage from Nico's temper. My rent here is so high because the landowner predicted things like this would happen.

I don't speak again.

This is fair. My blood took away Nico's mother. The woman I loved as my own mother is dead because of my blood. I should be witness to my dream of opening this salon being destroyed by my childhood bestie.

Nico peed his pants once when Daddy Valentino came home with blood all over his shirt and hands. I sneaked into his bedroom and got him clean clothes, never once making a joke of it because the two of us were in the same boat—the youngest kids in two families with too many dangerous secrets.

I am never allowed to speak in my defense.

But I don't have to bear the shame of my entire race, I remind myself. All I can do is all I can do, and I am doing my best to broker peace when war is always at the ready.

3

PEACE IS POSSIBLE

COLETTE

I do nothing while Nico trashes my salon, not because I can't, but because I very much can. I could shoot him with my non-lethal bullets. Sure, vampires heal faster than us humans, but a girl with a gun isn't who I want to be. I will not be my father's daughter. Not to Nico, at least.

I'm his pretend sister.

Or I used to be, anyway.

My heart aches but never breaks, even as I watch Nico smash my dreams with all the rage in his soul. I won't rob him of it. If it was anyone else, I would have pulled one of my guns and shot him already. But he's my Nino-bear.

And I was his Coco-bear.

I'm not sure if Nico decides he has run out of drywall or run out of rage, but finally he stops destroying my busi-

ness. His chest heaves, and for a second, I swear I see moisture sparkling in his eyes.

He hates me just as much as I hate myself for everything that has happened. Neither of us had a lick of control
over any of it. We were both left with only me to blame.

Nico is breathing in short pants, like his own fury has
been too exhausting to carry around this long.

I know the feeling. The difference between us isn't the
rage; it's what we do with it. Nico is bent on destroying my
family. While I can't blame him, my mission is to broker
peace, even if I have to walk through a war to get there.

My back is plastered against the far wall, my feet still
bare as glass glistens around me like the remnants of a
party I should never have come to. Agony splashes over my
features, marring the stoic demeanor I was trying to wear
like armor he cannot dent.

Nico is breathless as he meets my eyes. For a second,
true fear reveals itself only to me. Regret mingles with
horror in his features, stilling his attack, if only for the
moment. "This wasn't... I didn't mean..."

He's mid-apology; I can feel it. He is on the cusp of
understanding that we can do better than this. We can set
the example for how two separate races should behave,
like we used to do.

But his hatred of my family takes over, stealing his
humility and replacing it with hubris.

Nico kicks a chunk of the debris in my direction.

"You're playing with fire, opening up a business here. Watch your back, Colette."

I swallow hard, clawing for the high road, even though it is less appealing than punching him in the face. "I'll see you around, Nino-bear."

His steps falter at the childhood nickname, invoked like a plea to the saints. His eyes close as he braces himself on the doorjamb. "You don't fight fair, Colette."

Colette, not Coco-bear.

My lower lip quivers. "That's the thing about not fighting at all."

I will not cry. I will not show weakness. I will not show anything short of what I am. He has not earned the right to see me raw. "I've never wanted to fight you. I'm only in this for the popsicles and mud pies."

It's not a smile Nico casts in my direction over his shoulder; it's a nerve I've touched on that hasn't been exposed probably since I was around him last, which was when I was about fifteen years old. Now I'm playing the nerve like a harp string, making it sing for me to drown out the sound of separation that has fallen between us, whispering lies I never wanted to believe were true.

Nico doesn't say anything more. When he releases the doorframe, it is done with purpose, like he is trying to throw me and all I stand for behind him so he can keep his precious anger close.

I understand. Anger is sometimes more of a comfort

than a hug, depending on what you're looking to get out of life. Whatever he needs me to be, I will be that thing for him. I love his family that much.

I wish he could see that I am doing this for him. For Daddy Valentino. For Mama V.

Even for Rome, the older of the two Valentino brothers, who I am sure wishes me dead just as much as my precious Nino-bear does now.

I don't care that they hate me. I don't care.

I *can't* care.

I have a mission to make their lives better, if it's the last thing I do.

When I am certain Nico is gone, my spine slides against the wall. I gather my knees to my chest as my lower lip begins to quiver. Wreckage confronts me at every angle, my dreams crushed and crashed all around.

I didn't compromise my position of peace. Though I am proud of myself for that, devastation presses behind my eyes until tears form and fall. The drops of terror bury themselves in the silk of my blouse and the palm of my hand. My bare toes curl to get away from the world. I feel small and uncertain, stupid for all the choices that led me to make the decision to move home and set up shop in a city I unwittingly helped destroy a decade ago.

But that's not me. I swipe at the moisture under my eyes and will my spirit to settle. My dreams are not small, and I won't shrink them to fit the comfort levels of people who have resigned themselves to living in fear.

I cannot tell if my arms are quaking because my business was just massacred, or if it's my condition acting up, pinching my muscles to the point of pain. Either way, I know I need to take a pill soon to quell the shaking.

My trembling palm slides across the swell of my breast, feeling for the note I keep on my person, tucked in my bra, at all times.

Peace is possible, the paper says. I wrote it when I decided to move back to Mayfield. In case I forget why I am doing this, I wrote it down to remind myself of my mission.

That day, I hired a manager to take over my two salons overseas. I know I belong in Mayfield, where I am not welcome by some, and welcomed for the wrong reason by most.

One thing is certain; I am a polarizing presence. When they see me working in Midtown in full view of both vampires and humans, Mayfield and the world will have to make a choice: they will either bury old hatchets, or they will kill each other to prove their side is the one who has suffered more.

Clearly Nico has already made his choice.

It is an effort to stand, and when I do, my legs are unsteady.

I definitely need another pill. When I locate my purse

in my office, I slide out my phone and dial my favorite brother's number. "Declan?" I don't mean for my voice to break, but I don't hide things from him.

"What's wrong, Coco?"

So many things, but I don't want to look too closely at the details. "Remind me why I decided to do this?" I unscrew my pill bottle and pop one into my mouth, grateful the shakes will be gone soon, even if the fear never leaves me.

Declan's voice is calm when I am steeped in an unhealthy dose of chaos that threatens to tear me apart. "Because you believe we can be better. You might be the only one who does."

I nod, my eyes closing. I need to keep that belief strong in my heart when the cold nature of reality tries to convince me otherwise. "Thanks." I end the call and press my palms to the flat of my desk, willing my medicine to kick in so my hands stop their tremors.

I will not let them break me. Not Nico, and not Mayfield. I will rebuild, tapping into my stubborn streak, which has always served me well.

I will not stop until every business in Midtown changes their signs from *Humans Only* to *Vampires and Humans Welcome*.

I will not rest until there is peace in Mayfield, no matter who tries to scare me away from my hometown.

4

SEPARATED BY GLASS

COLETTE

I thought I understood what opening a salon stateside would entail, but I am fairly certain I haven't had a sip of water or two minutes to think about a single task all day. It's a good problem to have, really. There hasn't been an open chair yet, and we are five minutes from closing. All my stylists are booked for the next two months, easily. They are exhausted, I notice as I look around the salon, but their winded expressions are tinted with sheer glee.

You can't even see the holes Nico smashed in the wall last week.

The broom or the phone (sometimes both) have been glued to my palms for the better part of the entire day, and it shows. Though I feel like I have just barely contained a natural disaster, the place is spotless. My new customers are thrilled with their gorgeous hairstyles, and I am over-joyed no one has opened a firearm inside my business.

"I'll be able to pay my rent with four day's wages, if this keeps up," Victor tells me, straightening the brunette bun atop his head. "I can't believe how well this went. I've worked at other salons when they were opening, and no one did near as much business as this. Well done, honey."

My grin practically splits my face. "Well done to all of you. They wouldn't have booked repeat appointments if they weren't happy with the job you all did today, and every single customer made a plan on paper to come back."

Rachel snickers at Victor's elation. "This salon was either going to be a huge hit or a total failure. How many reporters were in and out today?"

I shrug. "I lost count. Eight? Nine?"

The problem is that not a single vampire came into the business.

But I knew that would happen. Just because I welcome them in doesn't mean they are comfortable frequenting a human-owned business. Trust takes time.

Rachel grins at me, tossing her inky hair over her shoulder. "Looks like you were worth betting on, Deadblood."

I hate that name, but I don't let my preference show, since Rachel doesn't mean anything by it.

Victor nods while he wipes down his chair. "I know,

right? When I signed on for this job, it was to make a statement, not necessarily money. I mean, vampires deserve stylists too, right? But honestly, I thought it would be a ghost town. No one wants to come to a business in Midtown if they might risk running into a vampire. And vampires aren't exactly going to flock in here. They don't trust humans."

Rachel cleans off her scissors. "Apparently all that's needed to turn Midtown profitable is to have a celebrity at the helm. Of course we're safe from vampire attacks if the Last Deadblood is on the property."

I grimace at their crass assessment. "That's not the message I was hoping to send. The humans are safe because vampires don't attack us for no good reason. If we act as if Mayfield is a peaceful place, then that's what it will be." I nod once, then reach for my statistics, which are always a cozy place for me to rest my brain. "Drug use is no different in the vampire territory than it is in the East End. The crime rate is the same, too."

Rachel boops my nose. "Facts don't matter when people are too afraid to listen to them."

No one cares about the truth. All they care about is that someone who is different than them seems scary.

My stylists don't have to understand my mission; they have good enough reasons for being here. One way or another, they all want the turf wars in Mayfield to end.

The sight of my employees warms my heart. We are all

exhausted but in good spirits. Two of the women are hugging each other, and Victor starts helping clean Rachel's station once his is finished.

This is what I want—team spirit that transcends a paycheck.

Plus ample paychecks for them all, which it looks like they will be earning.

I couldn't be more elated if I tried.

Rachel kisses my cheek before she leaves for the night, but on her way out, she freezes. "I... Um... Colette, maybe you should go out the back. Victor, could you walk Colette to her car?"

The fear in her voice doesn't suit the triumph of the moment. When I turn to examine the source of her worry, everything in me tenses. Despite the spike of fear in my system, I keep my voice light. "It's all fine. Rome is an old family friend."

I don't have to say this; everyone in the city knows the story of the two powerful families who split amid violence and deep-rooted hatred that sprang from decades of love. The head of the Valentino family stopping by a Kennedy-run business used to be a cheery, regular occurrence when I was little.

By the time I was a teenager, it became cause for gunfire and fleeing in fear.

Supposedly our families are at peace. At least, that's what my father promised me when I told him I was moving back to Mayfield. Though, it seems Nico doesn't hold tight to that truce, but sees it as more of a suggestion he can trample over whenever his temper flares.

I have no idea if that promised peace will hold water tonight.

I swallow hard, summoning composure. My father and Rome agreed to lay down their weapons so they could try to rebuild Mayfield together earlier this year.

I cling to that truth, hoping it doesn't fail me.

Why on earth is Rome Valentino here?

Victor stiffens, his nostrils flaring. "I'm calling Fintan. Your brother wanted me to reach out if anything like this happened."

My teeth grind at the notion that I need my bully of a big brother for backup. Of my two big brothers, Declan is wonderful, while Fintan is a jerk. "No need."

"But Fintan told me if any vampires stop by... And Rome Valentino is the worst of them all."

I hate when people use Rome's full name, like he's so scary and ominous. They don't know how badly he stinks at Uno.

Though, I haven't seen Nico's older brother since I was fifteen years old, so perhaps Rome has improved his card game skills in the past decade.

I keep my face composed. "There's no problem because we have a sign out front stating that vampires and humans are welcome here, remember? Rome is more than welcome to get his hair cut here. But we're closed for the day. All the customers are gone. If any of the Valentinos want to stop by, they can do so during business hours. Go on home. Everything is fine."

My stylists don't look like they believe me, but they exit out the back all the same, leaving me to deal with the vampire on my business' doorstep.

My chin raises as I silently dare the world to just try and match my kindness with cruelty. My heels click slowly as I make my way to the locked glass front door, studying the details of the man filling the view.

He is certainly Nico's brother in all the obvious ways: thick, jet black hair that is shaved on the sides with a couple inches of waves on top. Dark, expressive eyebrows. Wide shoulders that taper into a lean waist. Olive skin that is littered with a fair amount of scarring from a life lived outside the law. The head of the Valentino family bears angular features that emphasize his stern jaw.

I forgot how stormy Rome's natural disposition has always been. Nico was the juvenile joker while Rome never smiled. He didn't have the time. He was Daddy Valentino's top man, always going, always enforcing, always mired in the family business.

Rome's got at least a couple inches on Nico, which means he towers over me, even though I am still in my heels. I stare at the formidable man through the glass. He is backlit by the streetlights as dusk falls behind him, making him appear like a harbinger of grim things to come.

My gosh, he is more handsome than I remembered. Then again, he was twenty-five when I was fifteen. There wasn't much in my brain that searched for attraction to someone that old back then.

But right now, my mouth pops open at the sight of him. Flagrant allure burns through my bones at the most inappropriate moment, aimed at the person who shouldn't be able to evoke these sorts of baser feelings in me.

I push the fascination away, confused at my sudden burst of hormones. "Goodnight," I say, uncertain if Rome can hear me through the glass. I point to the "closed" sign and then to our hours, aiming a sweet smile up at him so I don't appear hostile.

I haven't seen Rome in a decade. Not since things got bad and I was shipped overseas so Mayfield didn't have to deal with me.

Though, I have always suspected that the real motivator for my move was because my father didn't want to have to deal with my condition. He signed me over to a nurse and left me to my fate.

Which led me back here a decade later.

Rome has the same Valentino ice blue eyes, the same intimidating set to his sculpted lips. The same lean yet muscular build, and the same ink-colored hair that nature would never dare let fall out, no matter how old the men in their family get.

I remember Rome well. Before I can stop myself, a memory pops up.

I remember a time that Rome was cooking drugs in the basement while Nico and I were doing homework upstairs. My pencil broke, so I skipped down the steps to ask Daddy Valentino if I could have a new one.

And there was Rome, cooking up what I now know to be a street drug called halluci-mend. It eases stress and relaxes a person, in lieu of mood stabilizers or pain relievers, which aren't always readily available to vampires.

I hadn't understood that the drug we were warned about in presentations at school was being manufactured one floor below where I did my Social Studies homework every afternoon. I'd revered Rome as the cool older brother who was always doing grownup stuff with Daddy Valentino. He was Fintan's best friend before the falling out with our families.

"Go on upstairs," Rome had told me, handing me a pencil from his pocket. "This life isn't for you."

Over the years, I've wanted to ask Rome if that life was for him, especially when Declan told me that after Daddy Valentino died, a new street drug surfaced and quickly spiraled out of control. The new drug is wildly addictive and dangerous. Its aim is to take down vampires this time instead of easing their pain.

Rome still makes halluci-mend, Declan informed me. The stuff he cooks up isn't addictive. It was largely created to relax a person and take away their pain.

The stuff sold now from competitors in the West End is nothing like the halluci-mend Rome's organization makes and sells.

Halluci-blend is a subpar variant of the halluci-mend that Rome makes. The newer stuff is sold only in vampire territory, aimed at those whom society has cut off and given plenty of reasons to feel miserable. Halluci-blend has many horrific qualities, one of which being that it can make a vampire's fangs fall out if they use it too much.

Whoever is making halluci-blend is aiming to take down the vampires and make it look like they did it to themselves.

The dirty trade devoured the formerly respectable real estate on Rome's side of town, leaving the West End of Mayfield a mess.

The humans blame the Valentino family for it, not understanding that those two drugs are two entirely different things. Daddy Valentino would never stand for something that could tear down his own people, as halluci-blend does.

Rome doesn't look as scary as I thought he would. Or maybe it's that I don't mind his brand of scary, since that's what I grew up with. He is intimidating, to be sure, but there's something to the way he tilts his head, silently asking me for entry that stills my dismissal.

I'm so distracted by the study of him that I barely catch the angle of his gaze.

He is studying me with just as much curiosity.

I roll my shoulders back. "We're closed. Sorry, Rome. You'll have to come back during business hours."

He doesn't speak, but studies me more carefully, combing the details of my face in the same manner I am cataloging his. He is every bit his thirty-five years, though time has only served to make him more devastatingly handsome.

Rome places his palm on the glass, fingers spread as he stares into my eyes. It's intimate, this intangible language we are speaking.

I want to tell him that his kid brother scared me. I want to make Rome promise that won't happen again.

I want to hear what his voice sounds like after all these years. Suddenly I yearn to know if it is still an octave below the others. If he still makes even the most crass slur sound like it's been wrapped in silk.

That doesn't matter. Or it shouldn't, anyway. Rome hates my family, and me, probably.

Then why is he standing on the other side of the glass, staring with such intensity? Why is his palm still pressed to the door?

I shouldn't entertain the gesture, but I find I can't help

myself. I move my hand to mirror his, though I know I should back away. Even though the glass is cold, I swear there is a pulse of warmth I can faintly pick out. His fingers are far longer and wider than mine, but in this moment, with no words, I wonder if we are the same—caught in a family feud of which neither of us wants any part. He was the one who went to my father to attempt a peace treaty.

Maybe Rome is just as tired of burying people as we are.

Or perhaps pride will lead both my father and Rome to repeat the bloody battles we barely survived.

I want no part of their war.

5

SCANDALOUS INVITATION
COLETTE

The corner of Rome's mouth lifts as he stares at me from the other side of the glass, but I wouldn't classify the expression as a smile. I'm not sure Rome knows how to smile, actually. I've never seen the evidence.

"Goodnight," I tell him again, though my voice sounds inviting, like I am accepting a scandalous invitation.

Which I'm not. Obviously.

I shake sense back into my head as I step away from the door. Once I know I am out of his eyeline, I shake out my hands, which have been aching for hours. My meds have kept the muscle spasms at bay, but I know that when my hands ache like this, I need to get home and take another pill.

I hope Rome didn't notice me scoping the broad measure of his shoulders.

What does it matter if he's sexy?

It's been a long day if I am entertaining thoughts like this about someone like that.

I turn around, dismissing Rome's presence on the sidewalk so I can retrieve my broom and finish sweeping. The shop is nearly ready for me to shut it all down for the night, but for a couple notes I need to leave myself for the morning. If I don't write my to-do list down, nothing gets done.

I don't need to worry that the head of the vampire family showed up unannounced after hours. I don't need to fret at all.

But when the door pops open behind me, it's all I can do to keep my shriek pinned behind closed lips.

I spin around, my spiking fear mingling with stark disapproval. "Rome, you can see very well that we're closed."

Rome looks just as sure of himself as he's always been, keeping a healthy distance between us. Still, his gaze seems to see right through my charade of control to the nervous girl beneath.

I hate that girl. She is the one who got abducted so many times. I'm not that scared little girl anymore. I am a woman with a degree and a business all my own.

The corner of his mouth quirks—still not a smile, but as close as he ever gets. "Are you closed? I would have thought you'd have special hours for friends and family."

Darn his beautiful voice. It's got a quiet command to it that bends my spine nearer when I should be inching away.

My head tilts to the side. "And which one are you?"

Despite his calm confidence, Rome looks tired. The bags under his eyes are easier to spot in the well-lit salon, though I know night hours are his busiest. "That's a fair question. I used to be both. Haven't seen you in a while, Youngblood. Last time I did, you were striving for your driver's license. I feel like you still wore pigtails back then, though I see those days have passed."

"Youngblood" is my least favorite name the media gave me, and he knows it.

I hold Rome's gaze, hoping my honesty doesn't sound like hostility. "If I wore pigtails still, would that have kept your brother from tearing apart my business last week?"

Rome's sharply angular jaw tightens. "Probably not. That's partly why I'm here."

I reach for the broom, gripping the handle as if I mean to weaponize the thing. "If you're coming to finish the job he started, I recommend bashing apart the far wall there. Nico barely touched it. You'd almost think his heart wasn't in it."

Rome shoves his hands in the pockets of his fitted black trousers. Nico's weren't nearly that cupped around his thighs. Or perhaps I didn't notice the fit of Nico's slacks in the same lewd way I am sizing up Rome.

He wets his lips, drawing my gaze upward. "That's not why I'm here. Or, actually, that's exactly why I'm here." He motions around the salon. "I stopped by to make amends and help clean up. Looks like your brothers beat me to it. Sorry about that. I haven't been able to get away."

"Shame," I muse, checking my nails as if this conversation doesn't bother me in the least. "All the best drug dealers know how to delegate."

No, I'm not about to make this easy for him.

Rome snorts airily. Again, the corner of his mouth quirks. "When you talk like that, I can still imagine those pigtails. Believe what you want; you always have." He motions around the room. "I can't imagine why you set up here, when there's plenty of real estate in the East End where you could have opened up shop."

"I belong where I put myself." I flip my brown waves over my shoulder. "I wanted to open up here because the feuding between our families is stupid. We're stronger as allies. Always were."

"Agreed." Rome holds up his hands in surrender. "I'm here for no reason other than to make amends, Colette. Nico was out of line to mess with your business. You have every right to open up here, provided you're not donating your blood to the Revolution."

I bristle. "How dare you accuse me of anything other than being used."

He motions to the family name on the wall in the

colorful logo for the Kennedy Salon. "You have the right to be here; I just didn't think you'd have the guts."

I roll my eyes and move to the check-in desk to put things in a better order for the next morning. My heels click on the polished floor, filling the space between us. "Yes, well, guts aren't dependent upon having a penis."

Rome's eyes narrow, though with the upward tilt of his lips, his study of me doesn't appear menacing. "Did you just say 'penis' to me? That can't be. You're twelve." He seems amused at my crass humor, as if we truly are old friends who can joke about stuff like that.

"I'm twenty-five, and you know it. Do the math. However old you are, subtract ten years and a giant ego."

Rome clears his throat. "Quite the mouth you've got on you."

"Came with the uterus."

Rome smirks at my sass. "I didn't mean because you're the only woman in the mix of the head families. I mean because the truce has been in place for ten months now, but no one has been brave enough to test it." He looks me over appraisingly. "Though, now that I think about it, it makes sense you would be the one to push us all forward. Your family seems to want to keep you out of sight. Your people either want to protect you or exploit you for your blood. And my people are mostly too afraid to go near you. Wouldn't want to provoke that notorious Kennedy temper." He moves toward me slowly and pries the broom from my fist.

He is close enough to touch, but I don't dare. I shouldn't want to run my palms over the planes of his chest.

Though my heart is jumping with nerves, I'm starting to trust his presence here won't lead to a scene like the night Nico graced me with his sneer.

Rome brushes the broom's bristles across the floor, meeting my gaze. "Well done, rising above your pawn status. Long live the queen."

It's my turn to chuckle. "I didn't know you were funny."

"Oh, I'm a regular crack-up. That's what they call me. Comedian Rome, cleaning up the mess his family made one punch line at a time."

He doesn't sound bitter, more matter-of-fact. Though, to be fair, he has every right to be bitter. His father passed down a mess, yet the world expects nothing short of a masterpiece to unfold, or the entire race will continue to be dismissed.

I cannot look away from the strange sight unfolding before me. Rome is sweeping my floors. I mean, the head of the Valentino family sweeping any floor is noteworthy, but sweeping the floor of a Kennedy business?

I take out my phone and snap a picture.

He speaks in a singsong voice without looking up. "What are you doing, Youngblood?"

"Photographic evidence of baby's first chore."

Rome snickers while he does a novice job of sweeping an already cleaned floor.

I motion toward the broom with my notepad. "You don't have to do that. You made your point; you're not here to cause trouble."

Rome waves off my dismissal. "I really don't mind cleaning up after my family's mistakes. I'm here to help, so put me to work."

And just like that, my hammering heart calms down. I watch him sweep, admiring the musculature of his shoulders more than I should. An entire minute passes of companionable silence, confusing me just as much as calming me.

I find I don't mind Rome being here, lending a hand while I balance the books. "I wouldn't say no to you wiping down the window and the door. Some comedian put his fingerprints on the glass."

Rome's neck shrinks. "Sorry about that. I'll fix it." He doesn't hem and haw when I direct him to fetch the window cleaner and a rag.

If this isn't the strangest day...

Rome polishes the windows and then starts in on the coffee table and countertops while I sit down and actually take my time going over the numbers. Then I make a to-do list for Rachel, who is scheduled to open on my day off. She is still learning the ropes of managing this place, but with a little guidance, I have faith she can do this.

Every few minutes, Rome and I share a smirk while we work in silence. It's actually pleasant, having him around. I find I don't mind the company one bit.

I don't expect conversation, especially from Rome, who only ever talks to his goons, and solely about blood-related topics, I would assume. But when Rome speaks to me again, my pen stills on the page. "Would you be opposed to me sending my guys here to get their hair cut?"

It's a bold question, holding much more importance than a simple change in cosmetic style.

"Beg your pardon?"

He shakes his head. "Maybe it's a dumb idea. I'm trying to think of ways to show the city that we aren't at war anymore. That might be a move worth making on my part. If you can be brave, I guess I can, too. Even if it means letting you hold a razor to the necks of the men sworn to protect me."

I'll admit, the visual dances in my head with macabre delight.

"It is a bold move," I tell him with a tease to my tone. "Political ramifications aside, you've never seen me cut hair before. I might be terrible at it." I'm joking, but I can tell Rome is finished trying to learn how to smile for the night.

"Forget I mentioned it. Your father wouldn't approve."

I bristle at the hard truth in his verdict. "True, but he's

the one who smoked the peace pipe with you. I would only be following his example."

Rome quirks his thick brow at me. "I'd really like to be there when you sell it to him like that."

I chuckle at the mental image of my father losing his mind to rage.

But this is the whole point of me opening a business here. I just didn't expect to up my game this quickly. The credo I wrote down for myself is still tucked in my bra. The words "Pease is Possible" burn against my breast with purpose as I consider Rome's proposal.

I tug on the ends of my fingers while I think aloud. "I want peace. I want the turf wars to end. If you're ready to make a big statement, so am I. It's my goal to have a business that serves both races. I didn't think you would be the one helping me get there, is all." My voice lowers as I hedge my bet. "But maybe don't send Nico here to get his hair cut just yet. I don't think my brothers will be okay with him stepping foot in my business for a while. You were right about Kennedy tempers needing ample time to cool. I'm sure you understand."

Rome nods, standing a little straighter. "Of course. Got any room in your appointment book for me?"

I balk at his gall, unable to help myself. "Are you serious? You've had the same barber since you were a baby. I thought you meant for your guys, not you."

"Scared, are you?" he teases me.

It's unmistakable, the lightness in his tone. Still, it catches me by surprise. It's easy, trading dares with Rome, who never trades anything without a hidden agenda planning his steps.

"I'm not scared to cut your hair, but *you* should be afraid to let me get behind the wheel of this thing. I'm killer with highlights and color. Not terribly well-versed in made men's haircuts that haven't changed since birth."

Rome shrugs. "I trust you."

It's a weighty declaration that hangs in the air between us.

I think I trust him, too, though it's not something I would ever admit aloud.

I swallow hard. "I've got time right now."

Rome leans the broom on the wall, mirroring my forced bravery. "What a coincidence. So do I."

There's a challenge mixed with newly birthed confidence crackling in the air between us. I keep my chin raised as I motion for him to come with me toward the back of the salon.

"Don't I sit here?" He points to the salon chair.

"I need to wash your hair first. You've got too much product in it."

"Sal never washes my hair first."

"I bet your barber also wouldn't dare tell you the gel you're using isn't doing the natural body of your hair any favors. Poor old Sal probably doesn't even wear high heels when he works. He can't be trusted."

Rome's upper lip twitches in clear amusement. "Fair point. Nothing fancy, alright? You've known me since you were born. I want to walk about of here looking exactly as I'm supposed to look. No highlights or colors or extensions or anything."

"No extensions?" I smirk at him as I select a shampoo for his thicker black hair. "You're no fun."

"That's my other name. No Fun Rome. It suits me well."

A casual demeanor slips over me, as it always does when I'm shampooing a new client. "Now, I can't believe that's true. I'm sure you're loads of fun. What do you like to do on your time off?"

He snorts. "Time off? Come on, Colette. You know as well as I do that's not an option for the head of the family. *This* is my time off, spent cleaning up after my brother's hot temper."

I turn on the water and make sure it's at the perfect warmth before I drag the hose over his hair. He looks so helpless, surrendered like this beneath me.

Well, as helpless as Rome Valentino can tolerate.

I smile down at him. "Not right now, you're not. This is your time just for you. Forget Nico. Forget our families. Forget the politics of it all. Right now, someone is washing your hair for you while you close your eyes and relax." I pause washing to move the footrest up for him. Then I whisper in his ear, "Close your eyes, hun."

He looks me over curiously. I know he's scoping me for hidden weapons or ways I might hurt him if he allows himself to relax. Normally he would have one of his men frisk anyone who gets this close to him, but as it's just the two of us, either he will have to take to the task himself, or he will have to rely on the unused muscle of trust.

I try not to imagine what his hands would feel like on my body if he did decide to pat me down.

What is wrong with me?

It's a solid minute of Rome closing his eyes and reopening them, trusting and then panicking over and over.

Finally, I resort to rubbing a soft spot above his jaw just behind his ear. It's the area I put mild pressure on when a tense client needs to relax.

Sure enough, it works even on the head of the oldest vampire family in the city. Rome's fingers lose their tightness, his hands sliding to his sides. His shoulders deflate in time with his next exhale.

I wonder if this is what he looks like when he sleeps, though hopefully without the wrinkle between his eyebrows that denotes a lifetime of unmitigated duty.

I let the warm water sooth him as I continue to rub that lucky spot in a languid, downward motion. "It's going to be okay, Rome."

A shuddering breath escapes him. It's so strange, that flash of vulnerability.

His lashes are long. I'm not sure I've ever noticed before, but they are dramatic and dark, commanding my attention as I lather him up.

Yes, it's the second time I am washing his hair.

Does he need it? Not really.

Do I need it? Absolutely. I want to study Rome up close. I want to lust in plain sight like the deviant I am.

It's normal for a client to "mmm" or groan while they are getting shampooed, but the baritone in Rome's exhale tells me he hasn't been cared for in a very long while.

I take my time on Rome as pity washes over the hardened parts of my soul. My nails scrape over his scalp, moving in circles as I massage from nape to peak, and then settle a soothing motion over his temples.

His lips part as his breathing evens.

Poor baby. I can tell he is exhausted.

It shouldn't matter that he's got a freckle on his plump lower lip. It shouldn't draw my eyes at all. Yet as I work on him, the tip of my tongue wets my lips as I study the swell of his. He's handsome, though that's never been a secret. The surprise is that I am noticing how desirable this man below me is, and perhaps has always been.

I should turn off the water, but my hands help themselves to their new guilty pleasure.

6

TAKING CARE OF ROME

COLETTE

I have never seen Rome relax. In my expansive memory of all the moods and positions I've witnessed Rome in, never has he ever been completely at ease.

He fell asleep on the couch when he and Fintan were supposed to be watching Nino-bear and me, but even then, there was still a current of anger to him, a need to be processing his plight even in slumber.

Yet as I wash his hair beyond the time it would take for a long shampoo, Rome seems younger, like he hasn't had the life sucked out of him by duty and dread.

I watch the muscle in his jaw tense and then loosen over and over again.

I want him to truly rest, even if it's only for a few minutes.

I know I shouldn't, but my fingers act on their own, as if

they believe they are smarter than the blaring alarm in my brain that tells me to back away. The massage at his temples trails down the sides of his face to knead the tension away from his jaw.

He needs a shave.

"Poor baby," says the compassionate side of me that comes out at the worst times.

I know Rome is dangerous, but much of my caution fades into the background.

My brothers and father inoculated me to the shock of violence when they took me shooting when I was ten. Toughening me up has never worked. I still coo at babies. I still wear stilettos and spend way too much money on pretty bras. I'm a perfect shot, sure. There wasn't an option not to be, growing up the way I did.

I lean down, whispering so as not to spook Rome. "I'm going to give you a shave. Is that alright?"

He responds with some unintelligible noise that I think means he's okay with it, provided I don't make him get up.

Rome is precious like this. I'm not sure there's another word for it. I want to prolong his relaxation as long as possible, so I walk with quiet steps to Victor's station, retrieving the shave kit and readying the cream.

Rome hasn't moved. His breathing is even and comes from his diaphragm.

The bib flourishes around him with a flutter. I can't

resist. I have to take a picture of Rome wrapped in lavender, looking so sweet.

I giggle silently to myself, and then get to work. I haven't given a proper shave in a while, but my sore hands remember the drill.

I should be on my way home, closer to taking a pill. My hands aren't as dexterous as they were this morning, but they aren't shaking, thank goodness.

My movements are mindful of the pressure needed to secure a close shave, while also not waking Rome prematurely. I wonder when the last time was that he slept so soundly.

The cream makes his lashes flutter, but he doesn't open his eyes all the way. "What are you doing?" he asks, his words slurred.

I should tell him again that he is getting a shave. I should walk him through the steps in case he's anxious. But instead of that, the unvarnished truth spills out. "I'm taking care of you."

My razor lifts as he angles his chin toward me. His expression when he takes in the scope of my concern for him is a mixture of agony, sadness and exhaustion. "What did you just say?"

I maintain the quietness of my voice, even as I study the concern wrinkling his brow. "I'm going to take care of you. All you have to do is let me. I won't tell your people you came here, and I won't tell my family. Not everything you do has to be political. This is my shop, understood? When you come in here, you're safe. You can take a minute for yourself, and no one has to know. Let your men come in here for the statement it will make. You come to me to rest."

He catches my wrist. "Why are you doing this? Why are you being nice to me? What's the angle?"

It's an effort to iron out the affront that threatens to rise. I don't like the insinuation that I need a reason to be a decent person.

But I know his question has more to do with himself than with me. "You and I are the same, Rome. Everyone watches every move we make, even when we're not moving at all. Plus, you and I want the same thing. We want the nonsense to stop. I am not going to kill you, and you are not going to kill me."

Though, the very real possibility of both those things has not been forgotten. The weight of our families' age-old feud hangs in the air between us, begging us to deal with all that it entails.

Rome nods once and the air lightens. We are not devoid of tension or reality, but we are not dominated by it, either, which is a step forward. I wasn't sure any member of the Kennedys or the Valentinos could reach such an enlightened plateau together, yet here we are.

"I'm going to be good to you, and you're going to let me. That's your new job. Don't suck at it," I tell him, earning a surprised chuckle from the man ten years my senior.

"You're the boss."

I'll bet he's never said that to anyone but his father before.

After I finish his shave, I guide him over to a chair in front of a mirror so I can trim up his sideburns and get a cleaner edge at his nape.

"You're not going to comment on Sal's shaky handiwork?"

I measure the uneven lengths of his sideburns. "Never. Sal used to keep pretzel rods in a jar for Nico and me when we tagged along while our dads got their monthly cuts together with you and Fintan."

"I barely remember that far back—getting a haircut with my dad. Were you always this sure of yourself? I don't remember you being all commanding like this."

"That's the thing about big men with big guns and even bigger tempers. They don't appreciate being told what to do when there's pride and family honor to defend." I end the sentence with plenty of machismo added into my tone.

"And you don't care about that?"

Rome only needs a touchup or two to update the style and make it more contemporary, not a full-on makeover.

I keep my eyes on the job while I trade back-and-forths with him. "It's hard to care about the greater good and your pride at the same time. No disrespect to our fathers, but I think they lost their way when they forgot which was more important."

I don't like speaking poorly of Daddy Valentino. My own father and I butt heads far too often for me not to have strong opinions that occasionally get voiced. But Daddy Valentino? I was his little girl. The only girl in both families. My father tried to make me into someone I'm not, but Daddy Valentino bought me the dolls I longed for and taught me about opera.

And I got him killed.

7

RASPBERRY CANNOLI

COLETTE

I swallow the bile that rises and the panic that always threatens to overtake me when thoughts of the people I love dying rise up unbidden. I miss Daddy Valentino every day, and will never forgive myself for being the instrument used in his murder.

"What are you thinking about?" Rome asks me. It's only then that I realize he is wide awake now, staring at my reflection in the mirror as I stand behind him.

"Stilettos and hairspray," I reply flippantly, wishing the bad feelings away as best I can.

Rome reaches behind his shoulder and cuffs my wrist, claiming it as his own to do with as he pleases. "No, you're not." He lightly tugs my arm over his shoulder, so my body has to follow. He doesn't stop until my eyes are level with his, my breasts pressed to the back of his shoulder. "Coletta?"

The way he twists my name on his tongue shouldn't vibrate through my body. I shouldn't lean in. I am close enough to smell the cinnamon of his breath.

He fed today. The cinnamon is always strongest when a vampire drinks their fill of blood.

Damn that freckle on his plump lower lip. I shouldn't want to touch it. I shouldn't want to be this close to him.

I swallow my nerves, but more rise to take their place. I don't want to be honest with Rome—mostly because being honest with myself about my guilt that's interchangeable with grief isn't something I have mastered with any sort of grace.

"Colette." This time, my name is a command on his lips.

Curse those beautiful lips.

Finally, the unpretty truth tumbles out. "I was thinking I miss your dad. He understood me better than mine ever will."

It's the least sexy thing I can think to say, yet it just so happens to be the truth.

Rome's lips purse. "You don't need to spend your time thinking about that." He releases my arm, and I get back to work on his hair. "Your father is a pain in my ass, but he loves you just fine."

I keep my mouth shut because I don't want to debate that point.

"You went all quiet on me."

I shrug, and then move around so I am in front of him. I want his sideburns even, darn it. I take my time leaning in so I can get them just right.

I don't realize I am giving Rome a clear shot of my cleavage until his mouth falls open and he wets his lower lip. The tip of his tongue sweeps that luscious freckle.

Heat rises in me as I watch his gaze rake over the full curves of my bosom, unable to look away.

When Rome realizes what he's doing, he clears his throat and straightens, changing the subject abruptly.

"What doesn't your dad understand about you?"

That's a very clear wet blanket thrown over any notion of lust rising between us.

Good. I don't know what's gotten into me. This is the absolute last man for whom I should ever harbor romantic interest.

I focus on our conversation as best I can while I cut his hair. The reasons my father and I butt heads amounts to a long list. Ticking off the items one by one would make me sound ungrateful, so I stick with the most recent one. "He doesn't understand why I needed to open my salon here. He hasn't said so, but he gets that look about him and changes the subject whenever it's brought up. Hadn't even been by to visit the shop until Nico smashed it up. He only shows up when there's trouble. That leaves little room for a relationship."

Rome gives an airy chortle. "You're telling me your

brothers are happy you set up shop here? I can't remember the last thing Fintan was happy about ever."

I meet his eyes, this time not concealing my sadness. "Fintan doesn't approve of anyone or anything he can't control. Declan is different. He's my best friend. But even he doesn't understand what I'm trying to do."

"That sounds hard."

"It is," I admit. "Fintan and Father want me overseas, away from all of the drama. They want me on a shelf, not standing beside them, like I know in my heart I should do." I set down my tools after making the final cut. "They don't want me to take risks."

"They're afraid of losing you, Colette," Rome says with a healthy dose of compassion ladled across his words.

"No. *Declan* is afraid of losing me. Father and Fintan are afraid of losing a war. Big difference."

"I think we're all a little afraid of both."

We don't speak of my abductions. We don't speak about the details of a war fought poorly and with casualties on both sides.

"My father lost me a long time ago." I firm my mouth. "Fear isn't a good reason to do anything. They don't understand that, so here I am, pouring my heart out to a Valentino in the middle of the night. Funny how life twists."

"Funny, indeed."

I clean up Victor's station while Rome sits in the chair,

watching my movements like he's never seen me before. It's strange, the way his eyes follow me. I'm so needy for a connection with this man that his gaze almost feels like hands on my body, warming and caressing in exactly the ways I've needed for far too long.

My stupid hands are growing clumsy, my fingers losing their dexterity. I knock over a bottle on Victor's station, but luckily the lid was closed.

Rome clears his throat and angles his face away from me. "I'm meeting with your father on Friday for our biweekly check-in. Maybe we should have it here."

"At my salon?"

"Why not? I'd be ceding homecourt advantage, so your dad wouldn't be so defensive. He might be ready to move forward with more things like this if he isn't so on edge, thinking the nearest vampire might up and bite him."

"Where are you going to sit?" I motion to the two cream-colored leather couches in the waiting area. "It's not exactly a big enough space for you, plus your security, plus my dad, and my clients. And when this place gets going, the dryers make conversation problematic."

Rome waves off my concern. "I'll have a table and chairs put out front, so it won't interfere with your regular business. Plus, it would be good for everyone passing by to see the two heads of the families hanging out, like old times. Might encourage more vampires to frequent your business."

I like everything he's saying, but hesitation still nags at me. "I'm not sure my father will go for it."

Rome stands, smoothing out his crisp white button-down shirt. "I'm not asking your father; I'm asking his daughter. This is *your* business, not his." His shoulders broaden, reminding me that he is every bit the head of the most formidable vampire family in the world. "It's your grand opening today. Best not forget the important things."

I straighten, my shoulders rolling back. "Then I accept. Just don't bring Nico around, okay? My family isn't exactly the forgiving type this early on."

"Fair enough. Just Orlando and me, then."

Orlando.

I haven't seen the Valentino cousin in years. I'm sure I am the only person who has ever been sad not to see the Valentino enforcer on the regular, but not a day goes by that I don't wish I could see Orlando and hug the scowl off his cutie pie face.

Rome motions around the salon. "I respect you for doing this, by the way. Never would've guessed that the youngest of all of us would be the bravest one. You're teaching me all sorts of new things, Youngblood."

I don't know what to say to the blatant compliment. I'm so accustomed to having to defend myself that praise hits my ears at an entirely new angle.

I suddenly want to confess that I am not brave at all. I'm terrified of being abducted again. I'm only acting brave so people assume it would be stupid to snatch at me again. I must have an ace up my sleeve.

In fact, what I have up my sleeve is sweat that comes from high rent and a twelve-hour shift.

Rome reaches into his wallet and pulls out a stack of bills, setting them on the counter as he readies to leave.

That snaps me to attention. "You know that's way too much, Rome." I'm not about to be a charity case (even though this is a new branch of the business, and we need every penny we can get). Still, I'm not entirely devoid of pride. I am my father's daughter, after all. I take out the cost of the cut and shave, plus a modest tip, and hand the rest back to him.

I hate that my hand quakes. I pray that he doesn't notice. I need to take my second pill now, or the shaking is only going to get worse.

Of course he refuses to take the money back. Rome's pride is just as much a monster as mine, once provoked. "Not a chance," he chides me. "Think of it as a welcome to the neighborhood gift."

"I don't want your money for that."

He narrows his eyes at me, as if I am an oddity he has yet to understand. "Then what do you want, Coletta?"

How does he say my name like that? It sounds ordinary on anyone else's tongue, but it drips with innuendo on his.

I fish around for something to lighten the mood. "I

want..." A smile sneaks across my lips. "Does Decadenza's still serve raspberry cannoli?"

He's so tall. Even in my stilettos, he towers over me with his sturdy yet leonine build. He stands close to me, warming my body with his, even though we're not touching. "They do around Valentine's Day. Good memory, Youngblood."

Youngblood. I wish he would stop calling me that. I loathed that moniker when I was little. My mother was supposed to be the Last Deadblood, but then I was born. So she was known in the papers as The Kennedy Deadblood, and I was the Kennedy Youngblood, ripe for the kidnapping.

Only when Rome says it, a blanket of safety folds around my shoulders. I almost don't mind the label when he is the one using it.

The desire to step closer is overwhelming but I hold my ground.

It's then I realize that Rome is studying my lips with the same lust that is wafting off me.

I blink up at him, though it does nothing to erase the haze of desire. "I don't want something as common as money. I want something beautiful and sweet. Bring me a raspberry cannoli next time they make them? Then we're square."

"Beautiful and sweet?" Rome moves his hand slow

enough for me to dart away if I wanted, but I'm not sure I do.

My breath catches and my body stills. He is the brave one of the two of us right now, because he does the thing I've been dying to do to him. He takes what he wants while I only dream about the scandal as he runs his thumb along the swell of my lower lip. I am malleable for him, my lashes fluttering with palpable desire.

"You're the boss, Coletta." His eyes study my lips in the same unprofessional way I am lusting after his. He mouths a curse word that contains equal parts frustration and reverence.

My breath quickens at the unmistakable tension in the air. It's drawing me closer to his body, as if I have been cold my whole life and am for the first time understanding warmth. It's not my overactive imagination. Rome's thumb plays with my lower lip with no trace of familial or platonic space. His fingers caress my cheek, stirring a darkness in the recesses of my body. His touch grants my spirit an odd lightness I did not think possible.

I shouldn't put my hand on his chest. Or if I do, it should be to push him away. But my palm needs to feel the hard planes of his pecs. I know the difference between wants and needs. This is an ache that will keep me up at night if I don't scratch this itch. It's as if his chest is the one thing guiding the way to a new horizon I have yet to climb and claim.

I am a mix of bold and shy, ravenous and wary.

He leans close enough that I can taste the cinnamon of his breath.

It's my turn for uncertainty to sweep over me as my palm slides up his torso so my fingers can grab onto his white collar.

I'll bet he's a dynamite in bed.

But that is not something I should be thinking about. He is ten years older than me. He babysat me, for crying out loud.

And more important, our families are deadly to each other. We are constantly on the brink of war.

Yet he lets me tuck the cash into his breast pocket because my left hand wants to test if my right hand was correct in its assessment that Rome's body is sheer perfection.

Both hands agree, but they want more.

"Mm." The sound Rome makes at my touch is low and sexy. I knew it would be.

I shouldn't be this close to him.

Yet when Rome crooks his finger under my chin and tilts my head up, I am helpless to resist moving my body to suit his whims. I am a sucker for a freshly shaved cheek.

I let out a heady gasp when he presses the crest of his cheek to mine so he can whisper the scandal we shouldn't be sharing. "I'll bring you something sweet if you keep looking at me exactly like that."

I balk at him, my cheeks flushing. "How am I looking at you?"

He leans in without warning and sucks on my earlobe before releasing me abruptly to drown in my pool of lust.

"Like I'm a raspberry cannoli." He reaches for the handle on the front door, giving me a clear shot of his ring that all the Valentino men wear with their family's crest emblazoned in the gold. His chest is firm and filled with the fullness of cocky delight that comes from leaving a woman utterly undone with a few sensual sentences and those damned cinnamon lips.

Desire rages hard in my veins, begging me to be bold once more and tell him to get back here. I need to suck on his lower lip.

Instead, I stand in the middle of my store in stunned silence, uncertain which steps I took tonight that led me to this moment of utter flabbergast.

"Goodnight, Coletta."

And just like that, Rome exits out the front door. He leaves me to wonder if I imagined the sexy tilt of his smile, or if the connection that crackled between us was real enough to keep my heart racing for the rest of the night.

8

DON'T BE DASHING
COLETTE

I grip the counter's edge. My heart races as I let down my façade of "I flirt this hard all the time. No big deal." I can still feel the caress of Rome's thumb on my lip. I can smell his cinnamon mouth as my own waters for a taste of his.

I haven't wanted anyone in a very long time, and even then, whomever my crush had been never got near enough to make my knees this unbearably weak.

I'm not even close to composed when Rome storms back inside a minute after his departure, his brows furrowed. He is folding a piece of paper he didn't have out when he left. He jerks his thumb at the door. "Are you in the habit of leaving your door unlocked? You can't do that, tré-sur."

I remember the authoritative yet romantic way his father used to use sweetheart names for Mama

Valentino. I've never heard Rome speak like that to a woman before. Then again, I haven't seen him in a great many years. Maybe he throws the term of endearment around like it's cheap candy for silly women to addict themselves to.

I straighten my back, pursing my lips at his harsh tone that's softened only slightly by the sweet name. "I was just going to relock it. You've been gone a total of one whole minute. And you're the one who picked it open in the first place, if you recall."

I pray that he doesn't notice the trembling of my hands. My left thigh's muscle is spasming under my peach skirt, making standing securely an effort.

Rome frowns at the handle. "Yes, well, I'll get you a new lock. This is easy to maneuver."

"I know. That's partly why I chose it."

Rome snorts. "You were hoping to be robbed?"

"Are you here to rob me?" I spout back, knowing that I must look like a flustered mess. I roll my eyes at his concern, pretending this whole endeavor doesn't scare me one bit. "I'm always misplacing my keys. I needed a deadbolt I could pick if I accidentally locked myself out."

Rome's eyes squinch shut like he is praying for patience. I had no idea the man was capable of expressing this many emotions in a single night. He pinches the bridge of his nose as he stuffs the slip of paper into his pocket. "I'm going to pretend I didn't hear that."

"Your hearing can't possibly be as bad as your manners."

He mimes a laugh, which I count as him actually being amused by my late-night humor. "Come on. Pack up. I'll walk you to your car."

It's my turn to frown at him. "Huh?"

"*Now* who's hard of hearing. I kept you here late, so I'm walking you to your car. It's dark out."

I didn't realize night had fallen, but he's right. I roll my shoulders back, feigning ease. "Thank you, but it's fine. I don't need an escort."

It's a lie, and we both know it. Most women might get a little jumpy (for good reason) going to their car alone at night. But I've had a target on my back since I was born.

Rome doesn't call me on my denial. He holds my haughty gaze with unadulterated steadiness in his. There's a silent command that the head of the Valentino family has always emanated. He never has to raise his voice. He doesn't have to hurry. Rome communicates all he needs to with a single look.

After a handful of seconds, my shoulders lower. "Oh, fine. But I can handle myself. I'm not afraid to be here."

Another lie, met by a cautioning tilt of Rome's head and a knowing look. Still, he's a gentleman who grants me my delusions if they make me feel safer. I need to believe no one wants to capture me. I have to hold to that hope, otherwise I'll hop back on the airplane and fly across the ocean to hide in a country that doesn't allow vampires or human radicals, so I can sleep without fear of being stolen away again.

The very real worries of the risks in coming back to Mayfield present themselves to me all over again. Anxiety tightens my abdomen as sweat begins to form on the nape of my neck.

It's all fine. I have every right to be here. No one is gunning for me.

My footsteps are quicker than usual, clicking this way and that as I hurry to shut off the lights and power down everything else. My thigh muscle is unstable, so I touch on various surfaces while I walk, hoping Rome doesn't notice me steadying myself.

If I fall in front of him, so help me...

For good measure, I check that the front door is locked, grab my purse and jerk my head toward the back exit. "This way."

Rome's strides are long, covering more ground so he can get to the door ahead of me. He pops open the exit and peers around the corner, reaching for the gun on his belt.

"Stop making me jumpy," I scold him with a scowl. "There is no danger."

Rome's eyes comb the parking lot, which is empty, save for our two cars. "Tell yourself what you need to. We both know you shouldn't be walking to your car alone in the dark."

"It's barely past dusk, and I'm fine. You know I'm a decent shot." Though, I'm not sure I could grip my gun right now if I needed to. My fingers are starting to go numb.

"I'm glad to hear that purse holds some heat. Where are your brothers? I'm going to have a talk with the sheriff about you walking to your car alone."

"Oh my gosh, do you hear yourself? I'm fine." When he doesn't let up as we walk to my car, I harrumph. "The more you worry, the jumpier I get. I don't want to think about the risk, okay?" I start talking with my hands, gesturing wildly the more worked up I get. "If I worry about who might abduct me next, I'll never leave my house. I can't live like that. Fear doesn't suit me. Fear doesn't get a thing accomplished." I motion to the building. "Fear has no place here."

Rome stops a few feet from my car door. He doesn't argue with me but waits for me to open my purse so I can fumble around for my keys. I know I didn't misplace them, but my fingers feel fat and clumsy now. My breath syncopates as all the times I felt eyes on me but couldn't identify my stalker creep under my skin. My hand moves more feverishly now, pecking through old receipts. I can't remember the last time I cleaned out my purse.

My mother was given purses, dresses and jewelry by top designers all the time. She was gorgeous and photographed often.

I bought my designer bag, saving my money until I could prove to myself that I was more than just a Dead-blood. I am a business owner. A franchise owner.

I have no reason to sweat.

And yet...

It's a whole excruciating minute before I feel Rome's hand on my wrist. His fingers are steady while mine tremble. He doesn't say a word but meets the fear in my eyes with calm control in his. He doesn't break eye contact even as his hand dips into my purse, revealing itself three seconds later with my key ring in his fist.

When I reach for my keys, he clutches them, stilling my hand. "Here's how this is going to work," he warns, a deadly coolness plaguing his words. "I'm going to get your locks replaced because those locks are flimsy, and you deserve better. Big risk takers should have big safety nets, so that's what's going to happen. I'll give the spare key to your father, so if you do lock yourself out, he can run it up to you."

"If I locked myself out, my father is the last person I would call," I admit. I chew on my lower lip. "Declan can keep the spare."

Rome studies my admission with unveiled curiosity, though he still doesn't give my keys back. "Alright. Next, I'm going to get floodlights installed back here that run on a motion sensor. It's not foolproof, and it's certainly not all you need, but it's a start."

A loud exhale of sheer exasperation stutters out of me. "Rome, you don't need to..."

With a small turn of his chin, my words trail off, giving him the floor. "And if your family isn't going to make sure you get home safe, then mine will."

My eyes dart to the shadows as my breath quickens. "You're doing it again! You're making me afraid when I don't want to feel that. I know this is the right move, and you're trying to scare me. I'm not moving my salon to the East End! I'm staying right in Midtown, and you can't scare me out of here!"

He hooks my purse around his forearm. His arms go around me, gathering me up in what could only be described as a hug.

Rome Valentino is hugging me. It's a leap from the reality I know, yet I am certain I'm not hallucinating. His words come low and insistent in my ear. "You're already scared, Youngblood, so let's be strategic about it." His body is just as hard and muscular as I imagined, but his hug isn't lacking in softness. "You know the risks better than anyone. I like that you're here. I like what you're doing with this salon. It's a statement the people of this city need to see. But when you walk into the arena, you have to do it with your eyes wide open and all your exits covered." Rome releases me from his gentle grip. His movements are graceful and unhurried as he unlocks my car and opens my door for me. "You did the big part, opening up this business. Let me help with the small stuff."

It's the least condescending way he could say his piece.

Finally, I hear him.

My chin lowers. "Okay, Rome." My eyes squeeze shut as I muscle through the words I know I need to produce. "Thank you for helping me."

"Was that really so hard?" He offers his hand, guiding me into my car.

"Yes."

I love the sound of his chuckle. I can't believe I helped bring the beautiful sound into being.

I don't expect his lips to graze my knuckles, but when they do, I am reminded of how stunningly handsome this man is.

I wish I could feel the caress of his lips, but my fingers are numb.

"Don't be dashing," I beg him in a quiet voice. "A girl can only take so much."

The corner of his mouth drags up, but then he turns serious once more as he straightens. "I'm going to follow you to the edge of the border."

It's not a request. There's no misconception that he will accept a world in which I might refuse the extra (totally unnecessary) protection.

"You're really that worried?" I measure my own concern against the crinkle between his eyebrows.

He doesn't respond right away but looks into my eyes with sincerity that cannot be fabricated. "No. You're really that important."

Do not kiss this man. Do not kiss him. Don't get out of the car. Don't grab onto his shirt and tug him down so you can do things you shouldn't even joke about with a vampire.

Rome winks at me, which sets off a fluttering in my chest. "Goodnight, Coletta."

I open my mouth, but no sound comes out. Even as I start up the engine, I'm not sure I will ever be able to make sense of this strange night.

Sure enough, when I pull out onto the main road, Rome's black luxury sedan with tinted windows follows at a decent clip. If anyone in the city noticed one of the Valentino vehicles tailing them, it would be cause for alarm. But tonight, as the streetlights guide my way home, the fact that Rome has my back grants me a measure of peace I didn't realize I'd been sorely needing.

Though this night has been the strangest I've had in a long time, I know I will be pondering Rome's protection for days to come.

9

TESTING THE TRUCE
ROME

*W*hat *was* that? I can't stop touching my cheek, even though it's been a good twelve hours since Colette gave me a shave. I shouldn't be thinking about her or picturing her face as she peered up at mine, but the second I'm not occupied with work, her heart-shaped face and plush pink lips come rushing back.

Orlando's voice jerks me to the present, however futilely. I've been distracted all night and morning, so he's had his work cut out for him. "Rome, what do you think?"

"I'm sorry. One more time?"

To his credit, my cousin doesn't tear into me, though I know he is frustrated. "Three halluci-dens on 6th street that we know of, dealing stuff we didn't make, so it's halluci-blend, not halluci-mend."

Nico talks with his hands as he stands near the window. "Who is pumping this crap into our side of the city? If they don't know what they're doing when they cook it up, people could die. Not to mention the entire drug trade used to go through us. This is a giant headache, Rome. With random people dealing this garbage product, we get all of the blowback and the mess, but none of the profits." My kid brother shakes his head at me. "This is what happens when you don't demand more of the sheriff, Rome. We need more help than he's given us. Loads more. I tried to warn you, but you didn't listen, and now we've got a mess on our hands."

Nico's lecture doesn't bother me at all. He's always shooting his mouth off about something, weighing in on the obvious well after the fact.

I wave off his arrogance. "You of all people should know that the sheriff's help isn't always helpful. He arrests the addicts but has no interest, it seems, in locating the dealers." I run my hand over my face. "This is our end of the city, not his. We will look after our people. If we expect humans to up and start caring... They have no frame of reference for that. I wasn't naïve enough to think it would all be smooth sailing." My gaze shifts to Orlando. "Are you handling those three halluci-dens?"

It's an unnecessary question. Orlando doesn't need to be told what to do. My cousin is always in step with me, making sure everything goes according to my plan.

Orlando nods once. "Of course. I'm dealing with them

tonight if they keep stepping out of line. Sent a message yesterday."

I love Orlando like a brother. Sometimes more than Nico, who's got a constant bug up his butt over just about everything. Nico's young still. He doesn't understand what I am trying to do.

Then again, Colette is his age, and she gets it. I have to stop making excuses for my kid brother. Just because his parents died doesn't mean he's allowed to be a perpetual punk.

Coletta. I can't place her perfume. It's flowery with a hint of vanilla, or maybe it's her shampoo. Either way, I went home smelling like her. I love the scent so much; I didn't shower this morning. I never bump aside my grooming routine if I can help it. I'm a creature of habit, and I like myself that way. But washing off the scent of her isn't a feat I am willing to try just yet.

I touch my cheek again and then covertly sniff my fingers.

Vanilla and flowers.

"Rome, what's your take?" Orlando asks me, reminding me that I'm doing it again—daydreaming about her flirty smile and our witty exchange when I should have my head in the game.

"About what now?" I hold up my hands when Nico scoffs. "Sorry. Got a lot on my mind."

Orlando hears me while Nico leans his knuckles on my

clean mahogany desk. It used to be my father's intimidating office in the upstairs of our massive home, but now it is mine.

Nico's displeasure is spread across his features. "Then give me something more than overseeing your deliveries. I'm sick of being benched when actual family stuff is going down."

I meet my kid brother's eyes with evenness, refusing to engage with his undying agitation. "You'll work your way up, just like everyone else. It's how I did it, and it's how you'll rise up in the organization. I don't want you falling under the weight of the pressure. I love you, Nico. I love you too much to set you up for failure like that."

I watch my little brother's jaw tighten. He grinds his teeth like I do when I'm stressed. It's a bad habit, and one I've never been able to crack.

"Out you go," I tell Nico, motioning to the door.

Nico shoves his body off my desk with sulky force, all but stomping from my home office.

I mean, honestly. If he can't keep his head when it's just the three of us, I cannot possibly put him in charge of anything truly risky.

Before Orlando can continue once it's just the two of us, I blurt out the thing I can't shake from my mind. "I'm moving the biweekly check-ins with Sheriff Kennedy to Colette's hair salon in Midtown." I keep my eyes from my cousin, focusing too hard on a contract that I couldn't care less about. "There's no decent place to sit outside, and I want to make sure we're seen being friendly at a Kennedy business. I'll need you to send a few tables and chairs to be set outside Colette's business for us."

Orlando waits a beat before answering. "On it. I didn't realize you'd moved the location. I'll have it scouted. Everything alright?"

I bob my head, trying to keep the movement natural, and not like I have an ulterior motive for moving our meeting there.

Not like Orlando would believe me if I told him. I cannot recall the last time I entertained something as juvenile as a crush.

"Just making sure we've got our friendly face on, so the Kennedys know we're not playing around with the truce. Colette's okay with it."

"She is? Man, I haven't seen her in years. How is she? Must be a pistol if she's set up her business in Midtown." Orlando's voice loses all traces of wistfulness. "Are you sure her salon isn't a front for Fintan's loan sharking?"

"I'm sure. I spoke to her myself. If it is a front, she's not in on it. It's just a salon. It matters that the city sees our families playing nice. I think it's a good idea for our guys to start going there to get our haircuts from here on out."

Orlando's thick brows raise, and only begin to lower when I fill him in on the arrangement Colette and I made.

"We're trying to firm up the truce by frequenting their

business in plain view of the city. We're not afraid of Colette or the effects of her blood, and the Kennedys aren't afraid of vampires. If we hold to that, the rest of the city will eventually fall in line. Then once the city makes peace, the rest of the world will follow suit."

Orlando's frown isn't unexpected; he rarely wears any other expression. But this one aimed at me is a little too pointed. "You sure about this? It sounds like we're walking into the lion's den with catnip and expecting it'll all end smoothly."

I run my fingers over my face, relishing the feel of Colette's handiwork. "That very well might end up being the case, but if we don't trust the truce, then what's the point of any of this? I think Colette made a bold move, opening her business in Midtown and having it cater to both races. I want her to know we have her back in this, even if her family is nervous about it all. She did something none of us had the guts to do."

Orlando doesn't argue this obvious point. "Fair enough."

The scribbled note I found taped to her front door when I exited after she cut my hair is still sitting in my pocket. I've read it at least two dozen times, studying the threat that boils my blood.

YOUNGBLOOD,

. . .

JOIN THE REVOLUTION OR YOU WILL BE SACRIFICED FOR THE uprising.

NOT TERRIBLY ORIGINAL, BUT THE POINT IS CLEAR ENOUGH: there are people in Mayfield who want Colette's blood so they can start killing vampires again. I don't care if she thinks I'm overbearing. Replacing the locks on her business and having motion sensor flood lights installed in her parking lot is just good sense.

It's my people I am protecting. It's got nothing to do with her.

Yeah, I stopped believing that lie this morning, but I still try to force it to sound true. In all honesty, I couldn't bear it if Colette was snatched at again. It was one horror when she was little, but after holding her in my arms? Even if it meant nothing to her, I don't do that sort of thing. I don't comfort women and insert myself so I can harp on about their safety.

There's no question about it anymore; I need to make sure she is protected.

Now that Orlando is onboard, my brain opens to include more details. "I want to add her salon to our patrol. Make sure no one's bothering her, alright? I want that business to succeed. Whatever her rent is, I want it negotiated down. Anything she needs, we take care of it."

Confidence surges in me, now that I can talk about her

freely, complimenting her, even. And I can do all of it without arousing suspicion that I haven't been able to stop thinking about how soft her skin is.

I lean my elbows on my desk, my fingers tented in front of my lips. "Her business has to thrive, Orlando. The truce is only as strong as the weight we put on it. Make sure nothing breaks her, understood? The longer that salon keeps its doors open, the more the city will start to breathe again. The vampires are always afraid we'll be slaughtered again, and the humans are always nervous we'll get bloodthirsty and start killing them. Her salon is one of the few places built to help us coexist. See that it lasts."

"Of course, Rome."

Orlando exits my office, leaving me alone with my satisfaction.

Finally, I have a legitimate reason to keep tabs on the little firecracker I haven't been able to get out of my head.

Though I know I am trumpeting the truce and praising the path toward peace, I have never felt more on the edge of danger as Colette's exquisite smile replays in my mind.

10

PICKING DATES
COLETTE

Of all the things my oldest brother and I do together, selecting dates isn't one I ever look forward to. "I hate this," I tell Fintan as I balance my phone between my chin and shoulder, even though he knows as much. "I don't want to go."

I open my closet and reach past my walker, which I haven't had to use in over a year, thank goodness. I grab a dress I don't care about.

Fintan snorts. "You know, if you whine a little when you say that, it might help your case. The girl you picked for me doesn't sound like a treat, either, but you don't hear me complaining about it."

"Um, I think that's what you were just passively aggressively doing. If I'm in this mess, so are you."

"Which is why I'm not complaining. It's important you find someone, Colette. You're not getting any younger."

I balk at him as I change into a boring bra. I don't want to put a second of thought into enjoying this date. "Excuse me, but my uterus is only twenty-five years old."

"Which gives you only two decades to crank out as many daughters as you can."

I blanch at words that should never come from a man, much less my brother. I stare at the light pink painted wall of my bedroom, wondering how my eldest brother and I grew to be this different. Declan and I are best friends. I'm still the only person in the family who knows that Declan is gay. What with Fintan trying to control even the rate at which I reproduce, it's no wonder Declan keeps the details of who he is to himself.

Fintan and Father have each other to keep them set in their ways. "Gross. The fact that every guy I go out with knows that is the worst. This is so forced. There's a reason why pandas don't mate in captivity, you know."

"It's hardly prison. You're going on a date in my restaurant. Best seat in the house. This guy is pre-med, Colette. He could deliver your baby."

I turn on the speaker function of my phone so I can throw it onto my bed. I gather my brunette curls up and twist them into a bun. "I'm not having a baby with this guy! I've never even met him. I've got a business to run, Fintan. The salon only just opened a branch stateside last week. I don't have time to put a pin in that so I can crank out a kid for the sake of..." I swallow the end of my sentence, because I know it's going nowhere productive.

Fintan's voice is heavy with disappointment. "For the sake of continuing our bloodline? For the sake of keeping the Deadblood genes going? You're it, you realize. You're the last Deadblood in existence. If you die, there's no weapon that can keep the vampires from rising up and taking over."

I roll my eyes as I slide the dress over my head. "That would be more effective if it wasn't the five millionth time I've been given that speech. The vampires aren't rising up. They're paying taxes. They're going to school. They're punching time clocks. It's not even legal to drink from anyone other than willing donors, animals or blood banks. Maybe it's best we don't live our lives with the sole focus of making sure we can exterminate an entire race just because they *might* be dangerous one day."

Fintan pauses long enough that I know he is gearing up for a lecture. "I sincerely hope you're joking."

My nose raises indignantly. "I sincerely hope the truce means anything to you, because that is the world we are living in—one where we don't have to worry about how to orchestrate the mass extermination of a species."

"You are so naïve."

My born and bred family temper boils as I wrestle with my dress, shifting it left and right until it is mostly in place. "And you are jaded, so you expect the rest of the world should be, as well. That's not me. I refuse to accept that your worldview is the one I should have to abide by."

Fintan pauses, so I know he's finishing getting ready in his house, too. "Well, lucky for the world, Dad calls the shots, not you. If I could procreate with someone and take one for the team, I wouldn't hesitate. But you know the venomous gene is only passed down through the women in the bloodline."

I grimace at his gall as I pick up the clothes I wore to work today and throw them in the hamper that sits on the floor of my closet. Tripping is a real hazard for me, so my floors are always spotlessly cleared of clutter. In my bedroom, there is only a bed and a dresser—no chairs, desk or nightstand. If my condition acts up, I have to make sure I don't fall and hurt myself on any unnecessary furniture.

I make a face at Fintan, even though he can't see it. "You offering to knock someone up is obnoxious. It's hardly the same effort involved if you're a man. And even if I did get pregnant, there's no guarantee it would be a girl. If my baby oven is anything like Mom's, I'll crank out two boys to one girl."

"All the more reason for you to get started early."

My upper lip curls. "You know, other siblings talk about their day or fun things they're interested in."

"Fine, Coco. How was your day?"

I scowl at the phone. "Shut up."

Fintan chuckles. "Actually, other siblings don't talk as often as we do."

"Maybe we should be more like them, then."

"You're being petulant."

"You're being controlling. This whole ordeal is controlling. I've had a long day, Fintan, which you didn't even care to ask about. I'm opening a new location, you realize. I just moved back to Mayfield and every single day, multiple reporters call me or show up at the salon. I have my pleasant face on all the time, and it's exhausting. I don't need you putting pressure on me and my uterus."

Fintan doesn't realize that I will never have children. I won't risk the chance that I could have a girl and perpetuate this curse on humanity.

No matter how hard Fintan pushes, I made myself a promise long ago that the venomous Deadblood gene would die with me. The world can't handle a weapon this powerful. They've proved that well enough.

Fintan's voice is even and adult-like. "It was part of the agreement. You move back to Mayfield, and you agree to try to find a husband so the family line can continue on."

I visualize how good it would feel to shove Fintan. "I hope your date is just as delightful in person as she was in her bio. She collects Pokémon cards, has a lazy eye and voted for the guy I liked in the last election, not the crook you liked. She also knits hats for her seven cats, who are named after the seven dwarves. Match made in Heaven."

Fintan sighs. "I don't care who you set me up with. Act out as much as you like. You're going. That was the deal. Dad needs you to go on these dates and one day pick someone suitable to settle down with. I agreed you could pick out my date if you did your duty for the family. And look at me, not complaining."

I've got enough on my plate without having to factor a dating life into the equation. I get why they think it's important for me to have a baby, but really, it's never going to happen. I made myself a promise, and I am good at keeping my word.

"Bye, Fintan. See you at the restaurant at seven. I'll be the one in the corner, plotting your inevitable demise."

"The reservation is for six, and you know it. I'll see you in half an hour."

11

THE SOUND OF YOUR VOICE
COLETTE

I end the call and fight the urge to chuck my phone across the room.

When the thing rings in my hand not ten seconds later, I decide I have kept a lid on my temper long enough. "You know what, Fintan? You're an ass. You and the sheriff can bite me. None of you want me to go on this date so I actually fall in love and enjoy my life. You don't want to be Uncle Fintan. The sheriff doesn't want to take his granddaughter out for ice cream. You all just want to make sure the Deadblood legacy is secure, so we have a loaded gun on the shelf, just in case." My temper cracks like a whip. I hope it cuts through the stoic non-reactions they always give me when I voice my unhappiness. "Well, I don't care about the family legacy! We're not at war with the vampires. If we truly believe in the truce, then there is no need to prepare for a war. Stop pressuring me to meet someone and get pregnant. I don't want that—not that you ever asked. Rome is in charge now, not Daddy Valentino. Rome doesn't want a war any more than we do."

When Fintan doesn't respond, I take his silence as confirmation that I am finally getting somewhere with him.

"I am not going on yet another blind date, Fintan. I don't care that the dude you chose for me is pre-med. I don't care how badly he wants to be one of Father's good little soldiers. I'm a business owner, dammit! I'm more than just a uterus, so you should be more than a giant ass."

When a voice deeper than Fintan's answers, I nearly drop the phone with a squeak. "And I thought my family was messed up. They really pick out your dates?"

"Who is this?"

I can hear the ease in Rome's voice, as if he's always known exactly who he is, and has never had to fight anyone for it. "This is the man who's coming to your salon tomorrow to meet with your father. I wanted to see if the table and chairs I had sent over to sit out front were to your liking."

"Rome? How did you get my phone number?"

"Are you seriously asking me that? Because I can do more impressive things than just track down a phone number."

I check my outfit to make sure I am dressed. Then I chide myself because that hardly matters for a phone call.

"I'll bet you can. To what do I owe the pleasure of such an illegal peek into my personal life?"

"I wanted to make sure the tables and chairs were acceptable."

I sit on my bed and thumb my white, lacy comforter, but pop up two seconds later, wondering if that is too suggestive a thing to do with Rome on the line. Sitting on my bed while talking to him feels...

What is wrong with me?

I shake my head at my fretting and don as normal a cadence as I can muster. "The tables and chairs are perfect. They even match the lavender of my logo. Tell Orlando he got all the details right."

"I'll tell him exactly that."

My mouth tightens. "No, you won't. You'll say nothing, which you think passes for praise. Orlando deserves better than that from you."

Rome clucks his tongue at me. "Talk back to your brother all you like, but no one tells me what to do."

I guffaw. "Do you hear how arrogant you sound?"

"Only when you point it out."

Touching my hair is a thing I do when I'm nervous around a cute guy. I scold my finger for twisting around a stray curl on my shoulder. Rome shouldn't fall into the "cute guy" category.

Since the night he stopped by last week, I haven't seen him or had any contact. His men installed a flood light in the parking lot along with a new set of locks. Orlando dropped off the furniture while I was out. I'd written off my crush on Rome as just that, and sent it to the graveyard in hopes I didn't waste my life pining for a man I cannot and should not pursue.

Of course, ten seconds on the phone with him, and all that logic flies out the window.

"You're being good to me," I blurt out without a lick of polish. "Why?"

Rome's voice is casual and laced with a quality that makes me want to lean toward him. "I'm not allowed to be good to you? Do I always have to be the big, bad wolf?"

When I don't have an answer, my cheeks heat unexpectedly. I feel like he can sense the effect he is having on me.

"Where are you?" I ask him. He sounds like he is sitting down. I wonder if he's at Daddy Valentino's desk in their mansion, or if he put together a workspace all his own somewhere else in the massive family estate.

"Where do you want me to be?"

If I wasn't blushing before, I am now. "I... I... I'm not sure."

His chuckle teases my insides. I love the sound that starts in his chest and vibrates up his throat. "You sound excited about your date tonight. Pre-med, eh? That's impressive."

I lay back on my bed, resting my head on my pillow.

"Yes, always impressive when your date has to send your brother his resume in order to take you out to your brother's restaurant. It's so forced, and honestly, I don't have the time for dating."

"I can understand that. You just opened up a new branch of your business."

A sigh of vindication inflates my lungs. "Thank you! I was trying to explain that to Fintan, but it's no use. So I'll go on the date and be in bed two hours later. Same Friday night I've had once a month since I moved back."

"Colette?" There's a beat of silence.

I am afraid to speak.

Rome's cadence lulls my defenses into lowering. "I had a good time with you."

"I did too," I confess. "You're not the big, bad wolf I remember."

"And you're a lot more beautiful than I remember."

I am floored at his honesty. I wish I could be that brave. But in my heart, I'm scared to anger my father that badly. I know if I say what I want out loud, it will be the sin my family will never forgive.

I can't even trust Declan with my secret crush, which is a first for me.

Rome sounds uncertain of himself when he offers up a quiet, "Coletta?"

"I shouldn't be thinking about you," I whisper, worried that if I say the scandal too loud, the universe will somehow find a way to rat me out. "I was glad you didn't reach out after that night last week. I could tell myself I was reading into things."

"Are you skilled at lying to yourself?"

"No. But I have to try."

Rome sounds at ease again, maybe even pleased. "You're only saying that because of our families. But what if they weren't an issue? What if I was a normal man who walked into your salon, having not seen you in years, and nearly forgot myself when I took one look at you? What if I was so impressed by your moxie, opening up that salon in Midtown, that I stayed up late wondering just how similar we are?"

My eyes dart to the door, expecting to be overheard. That's silly. I live alone.

"Rome, we can't talk like this. It doesn't matter that I want to…" But again, I cut myself short.

Rome's voice taunts me. "What do you want to do to me, Youngblood?"

My heart hammers in my chest. I move off the bed to check the locks on my windows. Even though my bedroom is on the second floor, I have to ensure no one can get near me to hear this conversation. It should never be happening.

I squinch my eyes shut. "You have a freckle on your lower lip."

Rome stops, and I can hear the squeak of his chair. "What?"

"I don't know what I would do with you if things were different, but I am positive it would involve sucking on your lip until I can get the image of it out of my head."

"Mm."

I love the sound of Rome's purring. It makes me want to stroke his chest—another thing I am not supposed to want to do.

"But none of that matters, Rome. You know we shouldn't be talking like this. You have your family to think about, and I have... I have a date."

"I want to see you again. Trust me, the more you try to put my lower lip out of your mind, the more you're going to crave it. I've been positively possessed by the shape of your hips, so I know what I'm talking about here."

"My hips? Men are weird. At least mine was normal. Lips are sexy."

"Apparently," he chuckles. "But there's a curve to your hips. They're just begging me to trace my fingers down them."

I touch my hip, dragging my finger up and down my side.

"Tré-sur, what are you wearing?"

It's an innocent enough question, but his voice does things to my insides. It makes me wonder if anything remains innocent in his hands.

"A dress. Pink satin. Knee-length. It's a Jé-Nor."

Like he cares to know the designer's name.

He hisses. "You shouldn't have told me it was satin. Now I'm picturing how it looks on you. How soft it must feel. You dressed up for this guy you don't know?"

"No. I don't like the fit of this dress, but I have to look like I'm trying. It keeps Fintan and my father happy-ish."

"I know that quest. It never ends well."

I lay back down on my bed, not caring that my dress will wrinkle. "I'm starting to realize exactly that."

Rome sighs. I can tell he's about to lay his cards on the table. "I don't know about you, but this sort of thing doesn't happen for me. I'm too focused on work to notice much else. But ten seconds with you, and I started to forget about all of that. I was simply myself for a solid half hour, which is a world record."

I roll onto my side, hugging my pillow. "I know the feeling. I stopped worrying and finally enjoyed my life when I was with you." I steel my heart mid-hemorrhage. "It will pass. It's a crush, Rome. Forbidden fruit and all that. I'll forget your lips soon enough."

Rome sounds stern now, almost angry. I picture him leaning forward at Daddy Valentino's desk.

Crimson carpet to match the drapes.

Giant mahogany desk filled with stacks of papers. "You're young yet, so you think connections like this happen all the time. I'm telling you, they don't. Not in my experience."

I close my eyes and wish things could be simpler, that all of this could be easy and fun, instead of frightening. It comes with the steep price tag of losing my family if they find out I am flirting with disaster. "I can't cross this line, Rome. I can't just up and do what I want. There are expectations. Hence the date tonight. I was only allowed to move back to Mayfield because I agreed to try to find a husband."

I grimace at how archaic the whole thing is.

Rome's voice is calm, despite the stormy implications of what this all could mean. "I'm not trying to push you into something you don't want. Say the word, and I won't call again."

I should tell him exactly that, but I open my mouth and the wrong thing tumbles out. "I like the sound of your voice."

I cringe. That was way too much to reveal.

Rome answers back with a casual, "How does my voice sound to you when I say that I'm not playing games? I'm going to start calling you at night to make sure you got home safe. I have it on good authority that you like the sound of my voice. Maybe I can give you some good dreams to hold onto."

I bite down on my lower lip, holding my pillow to my chest. "I might like that."

"Mm. Enjoy your date tonight, little cannoli. I want to hear all about it when I call tomorrow night."

A thrill races through my veins. Though I know I am doing the wrong thing, I can't stop smiling.

I end the call, blinking at Rome's number on my cell. I commit the string of digits to memory, because I know I can't put him in my phone as a contact.

No, this will be my little secret.

12

BAD DATE

COLETTE

I knew this date would be a bust before I even sat down. This should have been the first clue that I am not ready for this matchmaking nonsense. It was part of the deal, though, of my father letting me move home to open a business in Midtown. I'm supposed to start down the long path of finding someone, so our gruesome family legacy is secure.

We are at the table in the front window, so the establishment can show off that the Last Deadblood dines here. It will boost Fintan's bottom line, which he is always fussing about.

I keep my posture straight and wait for a camera outside to flash before I take another bite of my lobster.

That's right, Fintan. You force me to go on these dates; I will order the most expensive thing on the menu.

Thomas is fine, and that's exactly it. He's fine. Not exciting, not funny, not a single notable thing.

"Working on cadavers is a lot easier than I thought it would be. One guy threw up when he made his first incision, but I've taken to it quite well."

It's the tenth thing Thomas has been very good at, and I couldn't care less. He's getting his photo taken. The papers will speculate who my flavor of the month is now, and he will be interviewed by the Mayfiend Morning News while people tune in all over the world to see if the Last Deadblood has finally found her match.

Fun times.

"That's great," I drone pleasantly enough to pass as conversational. When the waiter walks by to tend to the table next to us, I flag him down. "Could you send the check over when you get a second?" Then to Thomas, I add, "I'm not much of a dessert person."

It's a filthy lie. I love sweets. It's my favorite part of any meal, and the only reason to eat dinner, in my opinion. But this man has talked about how great he is at slicing up a dead body one too many times. I'm gearing up to ditch early, which is right on time for me. I never make it to dessert on these setups.

Thomas leans in, cutting to the chase. "You can tell your father that I would be quite the asset if he decides to start fueling the weapons in preparation for an uprising. Tell the sheriff that I can draw blood in my sleep."

My blood. He's talking about drawing my blood to make weapons out of. He wants to dip bullets in my blood.

Thomas is not on this date for me; he's on it to further the radical agenda. He wants what the revolution craves: to exterminate vampires using my blood, since that is the most formidable weapon.

I stand as my upper lip curls. I toss my napkin on the table, letting the reporters on the other side of the window get the clear picture that this date is not a match made in Heaven. A few more cameras flash, but I don't care. Let them get every word for their gossip rags. "We're finished here. I'm not sure if you're aware, but we're at peace. I've never been okay being a tool to be used for war, and I never will be."

Thomas grimaces but doesn't bother backpedaling. "Sure, there's peace now. But you do realize that it's only a matter of time before the vampires need to be put in their place again. They're a violent species. The prisons are filled with them."

I should shut up. I shouldn't speak out against my father, but I can't help myself. "Yes, over-policing impover-ished areas will do that. I want nothing to do with your revolution. The world needs more people than just those who look, think and act like you."

Thomas' voice lowers because I am attracting atten-tion. "You know that's naïve. The revolution is coming. You're a key part of that."

Fintan can hear every word from his date two tables over. He sighs and waves me off, dismissing me from the ritual I want no part of. It's his surrender that he chose wrong when picking out my date for the month.

"Goodnight, Thomas." I whirl on my heel after outright dismissing him like the princess I was raised to be. Shoulders rolled back, I stalk out of my brother's restaurant and straight into the pack of reporters who all want their soundbite.

I feed them the same one-liners I gave them last month when my date went south.

"I am happier dining alone."

"I wish Thomas well."

"Please grant me a little privacy and let me pass."

Finally, they part so I can walk to my car, my stilettos clicking the entire way.

I am livid that this is the best candidate I attract.

A new, more devious thought occurs to me.

Perhaps Thomas isn't the best I can do. Glancing around at passersby, I reach into my purse and fish for my phone. I pull out the pink bejeweled device and dial the number I know I shouldn't.

When Rome answers with a breathy, "An hour-long date, and now you're calling me? I'm guessing it went poorly."

"You guessed right."

"Tell me about it, tré-sur."

He sounds out of breath, like I caught him mid-jog.

"No, no. You're in the middle of something. I was turned around, is all. I shouldn't have called. I don't know why I did."

"You called me because you like being near me. You were with another man, and it felt wrong to sit across the table from a man who isn't me."

I scoff, though he's not far off the mark. "Well, aren't you sure of yourself. Does your thirst for blood also come with a massive dose of ego?"

"In fact, it does. My swelling ego is only made worse when a beautiful woman leaves her date early and calls me because she just has to hear the sound of my voice."

"You're incorrigible."

Though entirely right.

"I'm sure I am. Tell me about your night, little cannoli. Tell me how I can make it better."

A litany of angry yelling erupts in the background on Rome's end.

"What are you doing right now?"

"Nothing important. Just... Hold on." He holds the phone away from his face, but I can still make out his authoritative bark. "Hector, leave the body there and deal with the ones in the back. I'm not coming here again. Take their stash and get rid of it. Flush it now. I don't want to see an ounce of halluci-blend anywhere in my territory."

I grimace, my neck shrinking as I get into my car. He's

on a raid, and I interrupted him. "Rome, don't pick up the phone if you're working! I'm sorry I called."

Before he can talk me out of hanging up, I end the call, floored that I would do something so reckless.

Of course Rome is on a raid. My father told me Rome has been trying to clean up his side of the city. I just didn't picture him being there tonight. In fact, after our encounter, I don't like to think of Rome doing anything even remotely dangerous.

Is he at a halluci-den? Is he surrounded by people who would happily murder for another hit of the bastardized drug that the West End can't seem to get rid of? I assumed Rome sent his people to do the grunt work for him.

The urge to tell Rome to go straight home and let Orlando handle the rough stuff itches my fingers, but I don't text the overbearing message.

Rome is not mine to protect. He's not my boyfriend.

He's not my anything.

13

CUTTING A DEAL
ROME

I can't remember the last time Orlando handed a task back to me. It's a true testament to how overworked we've been that he came to me this morning with the news that he couldn't talk Colette's property owner down on the price of rent for her salon. "I can do the legwork of trying to buy the property outright from the landlady, but it's a pretty steep price tag, and to be honest, the strip isn't worth what she's asking. Angelica said she'll negotiate only with you."

"I'll handle it," I replied over breakfast last week. Though now that I am headed to meet with Angelica Gilane, I have no plan other than to write her a fat check.

"Are you sure you don't want me to go in with you?" Orlando asks from the passenger's seat. "I feel like I failed you. She said she would only negotiate with you."

"It's fine. You wait in the car. Your shiner doesn't exactly scream 'fine dining.'"

Orlando thumps the back of his head against the head-rest. He is far larger than I am, so his head makes an audible thunk. "I still can't believe one of those bottomed out halluci-heads got the jump on me."

"You took him down. It was only sporting of you to let him get in a punch before he died. Then he passed on with a happy memory."

Orlando snorts at my attempt to cheer him up. He looks like me, only thicker around the chest and arms, and an inch or two taller.

He is the muscle, after all.

"I'll be back soon."

I've met with Angelica three times already, but she keeps putting off any sort of agreement. I can tell she is amenable to me owing her a favor if she cuts Colette a deal, but I haven't landed on her sweet spot yet. I throw on my black suit jacket and stalk into the high-end West End restaurant Angelica suggested. Why we can't meet at her office, I don't know. She likes to be seen, it seems.

Angelica Gilane is one of the few vampire women business owners who own property in Midtown. Every other stretch is owned by humans. It's a source of contention that she rents to humans who display *Humans Only* signs on their doors, but she is first and foremost a businesswoman, which is why she does so well.

When she catches my eye, she stands up and waves me

over, kissing me on both cheeks before we sit at the table in the center of the restaurant.

Ah. She wants to be seen dining with a Valentino. Some people abhor the idea, knowing it puts violent implications in the air. Others rush at the chance for the same reasons. Our money brings clout and stability that cannot be bought with fleeting finances. She's probably working on a deal of her own, and wants her notoriety established.

I've seen it before.

"Thanks for meeting with me, Rome," she says with a welcoming smile. "I ordered you some champagne. I hope that's alright."

Well, I hate champagne just about as much as I loathe someone ordering my food for me. But as I'm still mid-negotiation, I let it slide. "I assume that champagne means we're celebrating coming to an agreement, yes?"

She tosses me a coy curve of her red painted lips. "A date with you is always cause for celebration."

I freeze, barely able to piece together her words.

When I feel her leg run between mine under the table, I know I heard her correctly.

Dammit. I'm usually better at spotting problems like this before I'm buried this deep in them. I've been so focused on Colette that I didn't realize each delay in this deal has meant another date for Angelica.

"I'm here for business, not pleasure." It's abrupt, sure, but I am off the market. I was never on the market, even before Colette came into the picture. I am married to my job, but Colette has managed to open up my schedule for our phone calls. I've made spending time on her a priority—however small that window turns out to be every night when I call her before she goes to bed.

I am such an idiot. I could be on the phone with Colette, but here I am, accidentally dating the property owner of her business. I played this all wrong.

Angelica's smile freezes, but she recovers quickly. "I'm sure we can change that."

"I'm positive we can't." How did I miss her cleavage wrapped in red silk, aimed right at me? She's leaning forward, undressing me with her eyes while her foot travels further up my leg. I scoot my chair back, making it clear that I am not up for grabs. Had this been a month ago, I would have treated myself to a quickie in the bathroom with her. I would have closed the deal and left without a second thought.

Now the very idea sounds disgusting.

Angelica is desirable enough, objectively speaking. She's certainly more age appropriate. She doesn't have blood that could kill me. Her family wouldn't plot my death if they found out we were dating. My father helped her secure her property in Midtown many years ago, setting her up for success, which is rare for our people. Shortly after her name was on the deed, a law was passed that vampires cannot own property outside of the West

End, so Angelica knows what an anomaly she is. She is one of the few vampires who holds a position of power over humans.

And here I am asking her to lower her price for one of them.

Yes, my life would be far less complicated if I fancied Angelica.

But that's not what I want. It's Colette whose face keeps surfacing in my mind. It's Colette who makes me believe that all those complications which should keep us apart are mere suggestions.

But in fact, they are impossibilities that will never change.

I have fallen hard for my tré-sur. I am only here because I want to negotiate a better deal for her salon's rent. But turning down a woman whose suggestive advances have made it plain that she will let me do whatever I'd like to her makes it clear to me that this is more than an infantile infatuation I've got going with Colette.

My heart is sealing itself off against all outside influence and focusing itself on Colette's wellbeing.

I need to close this deal. New businesses are hard to get off the ground, especially in the first few years. Colette's rent is ridiculous. I'm all for our people taking their advantage whenever they can, but Angelica is charging Coletta nearly twice what she is charging the other businesses on that same strip.

A patron at a nearby table is reading a newspaper with my little cannoli's face printed on it. My focus is divided now, catching the headline that tightens my stomach. *The Last Deadblood Dotes on Doctor.*

Fantastic.

I don't mind that the papers cover everything Colette does. That's how it's always been for her. What bothers me is that the entire world speculates on her dating life because they desperately want her to settle down and give birth to a girl, so the Deadblood line can continue. It was the same for Mama Kennedy. Eventually she became a diplomat who advocated for vampiric rights, but when she died, her ideals were pushed to the side so everyone could focus on controlling the non-issue of a potential vampire uprising.

Give me a break.

I clear my throat, refocusing my attention on the matter at-hand. "I'm interested in how we can lower the rent for the Kennedy Salon. Let's talk about that and forget the rest."

Angelica picks up her champagne and takes a sip, locking her eyes on me while she swallows. I don't know how she manages to make that look predatorial, but it is clear she doesn't understand the simplicity of "no means no."

She reaches for my legs under the table with her foot, but I angle my knees away. "I already told Orlando, I'm not sure I can lower it much more than a hundred dollars a month."

"That's not good enough. We both know you're over-charging her business more than anyone else on your strip."

"Well, that's the thing, isn't it. It's *my* strip. I can charge what I like. It's a hot spot for businesses. Plenty of foot traffic. Midtown real estate is difficult to come by."

"How can we meet in the middle? It's important to the families that the salon thrives. I'm sure you understand what a big statement of peace it makes to the city that the Last Deadblood has opened up a business in Midtown."

She sets down her glass. "I know exactly how big a deal it is. That's why I can charge her as much as I am. No one else would lease to her, you know. I did a good thing—a show of peace, if you will—by renting to her in the first place. Her own kind wouldn't sign a contract with her because they don't want the responsibility of cleaning up after things go south."

My stomach tightens. "There's been peace between the humans and vampires for almost a year now. The Last Deadblood is perfectly safe in Mayfield."

I loathe referring to Colette so clinically, but that is the media's term for her.

Angelica's tone turns flippant. "There are always rebel factions who will come after the girl."

Girl? Obviously, Colette is a fine woman.

Angelica talks with her hand. "I'm sympathetic. She didn't ask to be born that way. She's got a right to open up a business, just like anyone else. But everyone knows that trouble always follows her. And I'll be able to cover more than my expenses when it does."

Does no one understand that Colette is more than a prop? More important than a mere toy to fight over? She smiles and the sun rises. She laughs at my jokes, on the rare occasion I make one. She debates ancient philosophies with me when I read my dad's worn books to her over the phone at night.

I lean back, making it clear I am not hanging around, even for a drink. "Bottom line, I want to know what it will take to get the salon's rent cut in half. That's the number I'm aiming for. Not a tiny discount. Her being here is doing more to increase the peace than anything else. Have you noticed how many more people are doing business in Midtown since she's set up shop?"

"Sure. But that's way too much to shave off her rent, Mister Valentino. You have to know that."

I run my tongue over my top row of teeth, focusing on my fang. "Tell me what you want, Angelica. Tell me how we can make this happen. I'm not coming out here again just to have you jerk my chain."

Angelica sets down her drink. "I want to be taken out. Once a week somewhere nice. You and me. That'll get the rent shaved down by a quarter, but not by half. I can't go that low. I don't care how gorgeous and important you are."

Well if that isn't the...

I run my hand over my face. "If you think I have time to take a woman out every week, then you haven't been paying attention. The West End is falling apart, Angelica. My men are the only people holding it all together. So unless you want the nice place I take you every week to be the nearest halluci-den while we bust it up, you're dreaming of a life I simply don't live."

Angelica's mouth firms. I can tell she is not used to being told no.

I pull out a wad of cash. That's right, I came prepared. Not to be hit on, but I came prepared to do this the old-fashioned way. "Here's how this is going to go. You're going to tell Colette that you're cutting her rent in half because you support what she's trying to do. Every month you charge her half, the other half will magically appear from me. Our little secret. Easy enough?"

Angelica juts out her lower lip. "I was hoping we could have more fun than that. But I guess it's fair." She takes the cash and tucks it in her purse. "I'll talk to the Youngblood tomorrow. You're sure you won't reconsider? I'll make it worth your while." She sucks on her pointer finger, fixing me with a look that tells me she won't say no to anything I suggest if I take her into the bathroom right now.

My response is to stand. "Good doing business with

you, Angelica."

She rises and moves to shake my hand, but she leans in and kisses my cheek, pressing her breasts to me. "If you change your mind…"

Angelica is striking, to be sure, but she's not Colette, so nothing in me stirs at the blatant offer of sex with no strings. Though I haven't even kissed my tré-sur, every part of me belongs to her alone.

When I get into the car, I feel like I need a shower.

"I can see you closed the deal," Orlando comments, pointing to my cheek.

"Huh?" I pull down the visor and peer into the mirror, grimacing at the sight. "Ugh. I hate when women mark me like that." I smudge off her lipstick stain from my cheek. "It's like getting peed on."

"Making out with a woman is a far sight better than getting peed on. Good for you, Rome. It's been a while since you and Denise split up. I was starting to think you'd given up on women altogether."

I don't correct Orlando's assumption that I'm hooking up with Angelica. If he is taking note of my dating life, that should throw him off the trail of my actual affections easily enough. I don't like hiding things from my cousin, but this is a crime I know it would be foolish to admit to aloud.

I drive away with far less cash in my pocket, but part of my soul feels settled, knowing Colette will have an extra reason to smile the next time she talks to her landlady.

14

HAIRCUT

COLETTE

$\mathcal{I}$ was expecting dreariness today because of the weather, but even though it's drizzling outside, the morning has proved to lift my spirits.

The fact that my landlady stopped by to tell me she was cutting my salon's rent in half has been the pep in my step, so much that I can't stop humming happy little tunes to myself while I cut hair.

I got through to her. Angelica Gilane struck me as the type who only rented to me because where I go, the cameras follow, and my checks will always clear. But after a gesture like that? I am well aware she was gouging me in rent, but she heard my heart when I told her my dream was to bring peace to Midtown.

She believes in my mission.

My sunny disposition seems to be contagious, too, because three of my four clients have hugged me after their styling; they loved their new looks so much. It's life-giving to make people look at themselves in a whole new light. Today I feel like a fairy, flitting around the salon, bringing beauty to the surface while my navy skirt swishes around my thighs.

I love this place. I love it even more now that I'm not stressed about making rent. My two branches overseas are their own machines now. The branch owners are never late with their payments and doing steady business has never been an issue. I was worried about the high rent and the complications of opening up a branch in such a polarizing area, but today all I feel is confidence.

Not only that, but Declan needs a haircut. My favorite family member has been busier than either of us would like, but thankfully he had time this morning for an appointment.

There aren't mere smiles but hearty hugs when he walks in. Though I saw him two nights ago, after this many years apart, we are still making up for lost time.

"I can't believe this place," Declan comments, looking around at my décor. "It's perfect. And the branding is spot on."

"If you think I'm going to let you distract me from the fact that you've got bags under your eyes, you're going to have to do a lot better than complimenting my business."

I hate that he works so much. A paramedic's schedule is rigorous and unforgiving.

Declan shrugs. "I'm going home to sleep after my haircut."

I usher him to Victor, who gets started with a shampoo before the cut. I love that my brother is in my store. He never stopped encouraging me to start my own business and then turn it into a franchise.

I'm in such a bubbly mood that when my father comes in twenty minutes early for his meeting with Rome, the dark cloud that always follows him around has no chance at dampening my spirits.

"Welcome to the store, Mister Kennedy. Can I interest you in some highlights?"

Every now and then, my father tries to bully my good mood out of me, but today he has no chance. My sunshine is far more powerful than the sheriff's constant storm.

My father snorts and offers up a wry smile. "I don't think so." He runs his hand over his bald spot on the crown of his head. "There's not much to highlight, anyway." He glances around, noting the full waiting area. "Maybe I should have made an appointment."

I pause, trying to figure him out, which has never been my strong suit. My father and I couldn't be more opposite. "You want an appointment *here*?" I point to the floor, perplexed. "You want *me* to cut your hair?"

My father's thick neck shrinks. "I mean, isn't that what you do?"

My lips purse as my spine straightens. "I can squeeze

you in." It's more grace than he deserves. Being near my father is a pain I don't like to quantify, but putting space between us is his crime, not mine.

"Thanks."

I motion to my chair on the end, confused that he wants a haircut when for my entire adult life, he told me cutting hair was a waste of time for me.

I bite back any vitriol that threatens to spew out at him as I sit him down. I crack out the lavender bib and flourish the apron around him, fastening it at his nape.

I glance around, flustered. I suddenly wonder if I remember how to use scissors.

A couple employees skitter to the backroom, making any excuse to get away from the surly sheriff, and head of the Deadblood family.

My father holds his hands up as he stares in the mirror. "Now, don't get carried away. My hair doesn't need anything crazy."

I do my best to ease into banter. If I focus on how strange this whole ordeal is, then I won't be able to do a quality job. "Now, now. You sent me away to get a good education. Don't you want to see my handiwork?"

It's a well-aimed dig that I shouldn't have done.

He didn't send me away to get a good education. He sent me away because I was sick and he didn't want to deal with me. I got a good education despite him, not because of him. He discouraged this line of work every step of the way.

The sheriff freezes but doesn't defend himself, which is an unexpected blessing.

Declan is in the seat beside my father, chatting happily with Victor. The comparison between my brother and his stylist and my father with his is night and day. My father and I are no doubt sharing a prayer that I finish this cut as soon as possible.

My father's hair has thinned more than I realized, and his short brown curls are dry around his temples. I do my best to teach him how to put product in his hair, but it's no surprise to me when my tutorial is met with lackluster grunts.

Declan can sense my stress because there are very few things I don't share with my brother. "Coco, do you hear that?" He points to the ceiling. "I love this song. But I feel like we can do one better than these lyrics."

It's a challenge I accept with a grateful smile.

We play this game often over the phone, picking a popular song and singing it with altered lyrics so the song makes no sense at all.

Declan bears no shame in his off-key singing when he changes the chorus of "I can't get by without you-hoo," to "I can't fly high without zoo-fruits."

I laugh as I cut my father's hair, chiming in with my own version. "I can't park sly without doo-doo."

Declan claps his hands while Victor snorts at the fact that his boss just said "doo-doo."

My father doesn't smile, but at least he is silent while Declan and I regress to the age of twelve without hesitation. We sing to the sixties diva song playing through the salon. I love, love, love it here.

I smooth the hydrating crème into my father's hair, not bothering to teach him about the stuff a second time or tell him that I made it myself in the back kitchen of the store. I always wanted him to try speaking my language, but in the end, I was the one who learned how to shoot his guns, and he still couldn't care less about my passions.

Victor finishes up with Declan as the two of them sing crass versions of the next song that plays overhead.

By the time I am finished, my father isn't looking with dread in the mirror anymore; his eyes are fixed on me.

"You're happy," he comments, as if he's never seen anything so strange.

I keep on singing, twirling his chair halfway around so I can make sure everything is even.

I don't answer his incredulity, but keep my good mood close so he doesn't ruin it. "Next time, I'm coloring your hair purple." I tap his bulbous nose with the edge of my comb. "Practically perfect. All you're missing is a smile. We don't sell those here. You'll have to make your own from scratch."

He takes off the lavender bib and sets it on the chair as

he stands. "If I keep seeing you like that, you just might get your wish."

Huh. I can't believe we didn't fight. That never happens. I avoid my father like the plague because I don't have the energy to fight with him anymore.

The entire salon comes to a halt around me. Without having to turn around, I know Rome and his men have entered my place of business.

15

A CANNOLI IS JUST A CANNOLI

COLETTE

By now I am confident enough to make it clear that *I* control the mood of this place, not them. The impending war that's always in the air whenever the heads of the two families get together is no match for my cheery mood.

Rome read me poetry last night over the phone before I drifted off to sleep. Nothing bad in the world could possibly exist after an evening that perfect.

Declan stands at my side, reaching out to hold my hand.

I lean up to peck his cheek. "You go on home. You need some sleep."

Declan's voice carries through the entire salon as he motions between the sheriff and Rome. "For the record, this is a bad idea." Then he squeezes my fingers once to let me know he doesn't like this.

Declan doesn't like the sheriff, either, but Declan is the smarter one between the two of us. He hides himself and keeps quiet. Father doesn't care what Declan does, so long as it doesn't blow back on the family.

"Good to see you, Orlando," I say to Rome's beefy cousin after Declan exits.

Orlando is the enforcer of the family, which is a role that suits him well. Of course, I remember back when I pestered him to push me higher on the swings, and he dutifully obeyed. He looks like Rome and Nino-bear, only thicker and with a few more visible scars.

Orlando doesn't smile, but he nods once. "Miss Colette."

I loathe the formalities. I was out of the salon when Orlando dropped off the tables and chairs out front, so I didn't get to see him then. I've spent years adoring Orlando in my memory, only to be sorely disappointed when reality seems to produce distance and stiff nods.

I try not to let my gaze fix on Rome, but it's hard not to stare. He's always had a commanding presence. Where the sheriff is the thunder constantly making a big noise to show the world he must be reckoned with, Rome is the crackle of a storm in the distance. You know it's coming, but there's a quiet comfort to the rumble that quells my worries.

I shouldn't notice the broad scope of his shoulders, or the way his torso tapers to his trim waist. I'll bet he's ripped under that white dress shirt he's married to. All the Valentino men wear the same black slacks and fitted white dress shirts with the cuffs rolled. The silver belt buckle is part of the uniform, too, though I can't say I've ever paid as much attention to their attire as I am today.

Rome is beautiful. There's no other word for it. The ice blue of his eyes and the short, styled black hair make him command the room without a single word.

Dang, I'm a good stylist if I do say so myself. His hair looks incredible, angled up and to the side like that, instead of up and forward as it's always been.

When Rome finally does speak, he addresses my father. "Elias. You're looking sharp. I can see your daughter's had a hand in your haircut."

My father's neck shrinks. It's positively adorable, watching them test the waters of amiability. "Yeah, yeah. Let's sit down and get started. Did you bring your books? You had questions last time."

"I did." I can tell Rome doesn't like me knowing that he asks the sheriff for fatherly advice about his business.

Rome's jaw tightens as Orlando hands him a ledger, and they make their way out the door. Before they exit, Orlando turns around and heads toward me, a box under his arm.

The sheriff stiffens, but Rome waves off his concern. "Peace offering to your daughter for letting us meet here."

My father nods, his shoulders relaxing. "Fine, fine." He

pushes the door open, and Rome follows behind. But just before he exits, Rome catches my eye and winks, letting me know that even though he's in business mode, the flirtation isn't over.

Pink colors my cheeks, so I look away from Orlando as he approaches. He sets a small white delivery box with the Valentino family restaurant's logo on the top.

"What's this?"

Orlando studies my moves for meaning, so I am careful not to reach for the box too quickly. I'm also careful not to meet his gaze. Orlando is Rome's right-hand man, and he is faultless at spotting secrets. I'm sure mine are obvious right now.

"It's raspberry cannoli," Orlando answers, suspicion heavy in his tone. "We don't make those outside of Valentine's weekend, you know."

"Oh, really? That's a shame. I've always loved them."

Orlando taps the box shut when I try to open it. Finally, his gaze connects with mine. "Do you know what Rome got Denise for her birthday two years ago, back when they were dating?"

"No."

"Neither does he. Rome doesn't care about gestures like this. Only all of a sudden, now he does."

"Huh. I guess our little boy is growing up." My chin lifts, daring Orlando to call me out. I know he won't, what with my father and Rome right outside. "Is it a problem that Rome is thoughtful?"

Orlando leans forward, his wide elbow on my check-in station. "You tell me." His finger jabs the box. "Tell me how worried I should be about this."

Orlando is the most solidly muscular of the Valentino family. Though he's got the black hair, blue eyes and stature to command a room, Orlando has a rounder face and a hardness to his lips that suggests he has never smiled.

Only I know he has. I used to tell him knock-knock jokes before I understood that not all jokes should end with "butt" as the punch line.

Aside from that, Orlando saved my life when I was fifteen. I owe him the absolute truth, but no part of me is willing to cop to it today.

I swallow hard, certain he can see my confession all over my face. I can't bring myself to answer. Anything I say will sound like a fib.

Because if I tell Orlando this means nothing to me, it will be a filthy lie.

"The restaurant didn't make these," Orlando informs me. "Rome made them by hand in our home. You want to explain yourself?"

My throat is dry now—too parched to let a sound sneak out.

Orlando doesn't let me off the hook, but digs the knife

in deeper, applying pressure because he knows how to get a person to crack. "Funny what concern Rome has all of a sudden for real estate in the area. My cousin has never cared all that much about this block, but he told me that if I couldn't talk the owner of this stretch of businesses to come down on the rent for you, that we needed to buy the property out from under her to make sure you didn't have to pay too much."

My mouth falls open in horror. A storm of emotions swirls up inside of me, each one fighting for first place on my features.

He sizes up my reaction. "See to me, a cannoli is just a cannoli until you pair it with something like that."

My brown hair is in a bun atop my head, but I suddenly wish I'd worn it down so I could hide behind the waves.

When I finally speak, my voice comes out cracked and mousy. "Rome is the reason my landlady cut my rent in half this morning?" I back up as the sounds of the salon all fade into the background. "I thought she believed in what I'm doing here. I thought I got through to her and she cared."

Orlando's lips press together in lieu of a response.

My hand rests over my heart. "Does Rome think I can't handle it? Does he know that I'm in over my head? Does he want to take credit for the business turning a profit?" I shake my head, my brows pinched. "Why would he do that?" Raw vulnerability shines out at Orlando for him to pick apart at will.

It's a mistake, letting Orlando see what stuns me, but I cannot cap my reaction.

"You tell me."

But I can't conjure up a single word to say in my defense. My gratitude for the cheaper rent is still there, but I need to understand why Rome would involve himself like that. Had I mentioned being in over my head with bills? I think I said something about it being a new business and money was tight, but I didn't mean for him to put the screws to my landlady.

I thought it was me who had put up a solid argument for why my salon needs to be here, and finally Angelica got around to seeing my side of things. I thought I'd negotiated my way to firmer financial footing.

I thought she believed in my mission of peace.

All pride and elation deserts me completely, leaving me bereft and empty.

Even worse, Rome doesn't think I can do this on my own.

Orlando taps his fat finger on the top of the box. "Careful, Little Kennedy. I don't pull punches when people play with fire around Rome."

I'm not sure if it's a threat or a fact. Probably both. Either way, my stomach is in knots.

Then Orlando leans in, lowering his voice to allow a

sliver of softness to infiltrate his harsh demeanor. "You are not this naïve, Coco. Do not fall for this. Rome is playing you, sending you treats like these. He just hooked up with your landlady yesterday. That's why she dropped your rent. Rome wants you here to help establish the peace, sure, but he shouldn't be stringing you along."

My whole body is cold. Orlando's words douse me in ice.

Is that what this is?

My reply comes in a hoarse whisper. "What possible reason would he have for doing that? Why do you think he would try to make me all giggly and gooey for him? That's not exactly going to make peace for the families."

Orlando glances around to make sure no one is listening in. "A while ago, your father shorted Rome on a deal. The sheriff was supposed to send us some men to help clean out the drug dealers from the West End. All he managed to do was arrest more addicts, which is hardly helpful. We want the problem stopped at the source, not for vampires to be paraded around in cuffs for the press to pick us apart more than they already do. Rome promised the sheriff the money for a few new squad cars in exchange for his help getting to the bottom of things—a negotiation we shouldn't have had to do, since law enforcement is your father's entire job. We made good on our end of things, but your father never came through. We lost two of our men on raids where we thought we had backup, but it didn't come."

A knife slices clean through my optimism. Pressure begins to build behind my eyes.

I am naïve.

I turn my chin away because I will be damned if I let Orlando see me cry. "I didn't know that. I wasn't living in Mayfield when that happened. I've only been back a couple months."

Orlando has few expressions, but I can make out pity easily enough. "I figured. Rome was angry for a long time about that. What better way to get back at the sheriff than to play with his daughter's heart?" He shakes his head. "I wouldn't care if it was anybody else, but you've been jerked around enough in your life. That should never come from our family. I'm not about to stand up to Rome and tell him he's wrong to be screwing with you like this. I figure that's something you might want to do yourself."

I swallow the lump in my throat, unable to speak through my shock. I mouth a simple, "thank you," before stepping back from the desk. I snatch up the box and whirl around, ignoring the bustle of the salon as I dart into my office and lock the door behind me.

I press my back to the door and sink down, cuddling the square box. I can't bring myself to open it.

Rome went on a date with my landlady and then read

me poetry after he polished her off. It's hard to wrap my mind around it all being a ploy to get back at my father.

Then again, imagining that Rome wants to be with me has been a hard sell to my logical self this entire time.

Orlando doesn't lie. Not to me. I can still picture his round face when he rescued me from the basement where I'd been stashed when I was only fifteen. I couldn't lift my head; they'd taken so much blood. Orlando carried me out of the basement, past the bodies he and the guys had shot in their quest to get to me. He drove me straight to the hospital, making sure my family met us there. Never once did he tell me everything was going to be alright.

It wasn't.

It still isn't.

He pushed me on the swings when I was still in pigtails. Orlando didn't save my life just to watch his cousin obliterate my heart.

Damn these raspberry cannoli.

I didn't know Rome baked. I guess there's a lot I don't know about him. My heart jumps when I open the lid of the bakery box and find three raspberry cannoli in a neat little row. They're perfectly imperfect. I can tell they are handmade by someone who is no stranger to the finer things. My knees curl to my chest as I take a single pastry out of the box and set the other two aside. My short navy skirt slips up my thighs while I sniff the confection.

The very first bite takes me back to my childhood, to a

simpler time when I didn't know the difference between what should be, what could be, and what can never be.

No man has ever made cannoli for me before.

A swarm of emotions battles in my chest. Rome wants to get laid. These cannoli are bait for sex, so he can shove it in my father's face and break what's left of the sheriff's shriveled heart.

He's hooking up with Angelica, my landlady.

Suddenly, my appetite is gone. She's a real woman who's owned property and done business things for at least a decade longer than I have, if not more.

If I wasn't so head over heels for the man, I might be grateful he went to such lengths to ensure my second month in business wasn't the stress fest I was anticipating it would be.

But a sadder, more damning thought chases on the heels of any trace of optimism: Rome doesn't think I can do this. He doesn't think I can run the salon. He got his girlfriend to feel sorry for me and lower the price. I'll bet they had a good laugh about my stupid crush.

I'm a charity case.

Or worse, Rome wants something. Doom hits me square in the chest when I know I've settled on the heart of the matter. Valentinos don't do a favor for nothing. Same goes for my family, so I know the drill. He wouldn't lower my rent, then have Orlando just so happen to mention it to me for no reason. He wants me in his pocket.

Rome is playing me.

Two tears roll down my cheeks, and I hate them both.

I am stupid for letting things go this far. Rome reads to me over the phone every night before I go to sleep. I am such an idiot that I allowed romance to seep into my home.

I swipe at my tears and command the others not to fall.

I am my father's daughter—cold and detached. I have been through way worse than a broken heart. This is not worth my tears.

Except no matter how firmly I tell myself this, they begin to fall without discretion for my pride.

I put down the box of cannoli, losing my taste for anything sweet. I don't want to admit how hurt I am. I've been falling for Rome without a safety net, lowering my guard by inches every time he says something charming.

I sob into my hand, knowing I have been played.

I am the worst kind of cliché—a woman playing into the mafia king's hands, lured by sweet nothings until she is so deep in his pocket, she forgets her own name.

Kennedy. That's my name. He's only toying with me so he can stick it to my father.

Another tear falls down my cheek. I'm not sure if I am devasted that I fell for it all, or if I am more distraught that this means the fairytale has to end.

I always knew one day I would have to let Rome go. I just wasn't expecting it to feel like this.

16

ROME'S AGENDA
COLETTE

I've barely finished crying when my father's heavy fist bangs on my office door. I know the echo of his knock well. It sounds of weariness and anger, no matter the thickness of the door.

I stand up, casting around the modest four corners for a place to hide my contraband. "Just a minute!" I cringe at how guilty I sound. It's not like I'm holding something dangerous or illegal.

Though, I'm sure my father would prefer either of those options to a token of affection from a Valentino. This is exactly what Rome wants—for the sheriff to see me pining over a romantic gift from the rival family. It would break my father's heart.

Frantic, I stash the box behind a shipment of disinfectant. I swipe at my eyes, knowing there is precious little I can do to conceal the obvious fact that I have been crying. I smooth my hand over my fitted cream blouse and mid-thigh length navy skirt. I hope I'm not giving off any tell-tale signals that I am betraying the family by flirting with the enemy.

Only we're not enemies. At least, that's what the truce is supposed to communicate.

I open the door, unable to produce even a shadow of a smile. "Hi, I..." I stop short, surprised when Rome is beside him, looking all no-nonsense, as usual. "What can I help you with, gentlemen?"

My father comes in and makes himself at home, sitting in *my* chair at *my* desk. He will always be the biggest presence in whatever room he enters, including my office. "Rome and I were talking, and I had an idea. You opening up a business in Midtown is a statement, sure. Us having our biweekly meetings on your property is a good show to the city that our truce is firm. But what would take it further would be if Rome's men started getting their hair cut here."

I fight the urge to roll my eyes.

To his credit, Rome's mouth doesn't twitch. Of course Rome would leave a trail of breadcrumbs for my father to follow, making the sheriff think he himself came up with the whole plan. Lo and behold, my father's ego showed up to play right into his capable, cannoli-making hands.

Like daughter like father, I guess.

I cross my arms over my bosom, tapping my lavender

stiletto. The whole idea is bothersome to me now. I don't want to see Rome if I don't have to. Not after this. "Why, again?"

"If the city sees the Valentino organization frequenting a Kennedy business and there's no hint of bloodshed, it'll fast track us to a place where the old feuds can be forgotten. You know the vampires look to the Valentino family to show them the way."

I don't respond right away. The fact of the matter is that Rome has already involved himself in my business, which feels like a power play move. I've seen the sheriff do it loads of times—help someone get a break on some violation, so they feel they owe us loyalty and favors. Fintan is just as bad with his loan sharking.

I don't want to owe Rome anything.

I don't want to think about Rome involving himself in my life just to rub my crush in my father's face.

I try to draw myself up, even though I am the shortest person in the room.

I am five feet tall, so I am the shortest person in most rooms.

I raise my chin. "Let me sleep on it."

Rome frowns, his mouth in a hard line as his brows push together. "There's no downside. You'll get consistent business from us." I can practically hear the words he cannot say in front of my father: *We already talked about this.*

The sheriff's phone rings, and he takes the call while Rome stares me down.

I pretend not to notice, just like I pretend I wasn't crying. "I assume the offer will still be up for discussion tomorrow? This isn't a limited-time deal, right?"

"No, I guess not. I just don't see what the problem is." Rome studies my hesitance regarding the issue we thought up together. I can tell he wants to get answers out of me, but he won't demand them because the sheriff is sitting right there.

When my dad stands, he pockets his phone and moves toward the door. He pauses on his way out, as if he means to kiss the top of my head.

I glance up at him in confusion, my upper lip curled.

We don't do that. Declan and I hug every time we see each other and hold hands when we're afraid. But that is not something we learned from our father.

The sheriff grimaces, then gives me a weird bob of his head. "Give the matter some thought, Coco. This little shop of yours could use the Valentino seal of approval. Then it'll be packed."

It already is booked solid for weeks.

And it's not a little shop. This is the third branch of a franchise that I started without his help or input. He's always looking for ways to demean me.

Even though I am wearing stilettos, I am still shorter than him. I will always be shorter than him.

I feel idiotic and small. Gullible and childish.

My father doesn't notice my smashed heart. Those sorts of things tend to go over his head. "I've got to see to something on our side of town. Rome, fill Coco in on the rest of the details. Make this happen, Son."

Rome straightens at the familial address. "Of course, Sheriff. Can you tell Orlando I'll be out in a bit? I want to pitch your plan to the boss one more time."

"Will do." My father puts his hand on the doorknob but pauses to meet my gaze before he exits. "Just to be clear, you're doing this. Talk it out all you want, but this is happening. Don't be stubborn just because it's my idea. It's a good one, and something that furthers the truce you believe in. Save your bullheadedness for something less important. Real grownups are doing real work. Join us when you're done throwing whatever this latest fit is."

I indulge in a snarl, but that's the most I will talk back once my father has laid down the law.

And in front of a Valentino, no less.

17

COMING CLEAN

COLETTE

The second he leaves, Rome's shoulders lower. He makes sure my door is shut and then turns the lock. "That was all a show, right? You're making him sweat but you're still on board with the idea."

I cross the quaint room to my desk, straightening the papers my father messed up. "A funny thing happened this morning. Do you want to guess what it was?" I keep my face turned from his, maintaining my cool demeanor even though we are alone.

We're never alone. We're always on the phone, far away from each other. Since I cut his hair that first night that started all of this, we have been fanning our flame over the phone but not in person.

Rome throws his hands up, finally giving into expressing his personality now that it's just the two of us.

"Not a clue. Is something wrong? Because talking to the back of your head isn't what I was hoping for."

"My landlady stopped by to let me know that my rent was being cut in half. Strange, huh?"

Rome isn't dumb enough to play stupid. He knows what a mistake that would be. Instead of copping to it, he goes silent, playing possum to see how far that gets him.

Even though I am facing away from him, I talk with my free hand while straightening the papers on my desk with the other. "See, I'm trying to think of why Angelica would do that. Then Orlando comes in and drops off the best raspberry cannoli in the world, along with the news that you are the force behind your girlfriend's sudden benevolence. What I don't understand is why. What's your angle, Valentino?"

"My angle?" His face sours. "Wait, you think I have a girlfriend? You think Angelica is my girlfriend?"

"I've seen this game. I know what happens next. You get me a deal on my rent. Then when you need a favor from me, I'm obligated to jump to your whistle. So just tell me now—what's this going to cost me?"

Rome runs his hand over his mouth, sizing me up in a new light. "I guess we are a perfect match; you're just as jaded as I am."

"I was raised knowing the rules, just like you were. What I don't get is why the flirtation? Why toy with me if all you had to do was cut my rent in half to buy my loyalty?

Why make me raspberry cannoli and call me and make me want..." I feel stupid for not seeing it all clearer from the beginning. Even stupider because my voice is catching with emotion that I don't want to show him. A man who does this to me doesn't deserve to see me raw and breakable. Rarely have I tolerated being either of those things. "You're trying to stick it to my family by getting me to fall for you. Orlando explained it all to me."

He fixes me with a hollow stare. "Orlando said what?"

I sniffle back my heartbreak. "It's the only thing that makes sense. And frankly, it's beneath you."

There's a weighty pause before Rome speaks in his cool, authoritative manner. "Sit down."

I turn to look him up and down, fixing him with my coldest stare. "I know you're not trying to tell me what to do."

His eyes close in veiled frustration. "Please have a seat with me, Colette. I'm not leaving until we hash this out."

I comply and I take the chair behind my desk, leaving the guest seat for him. It's bad enough that my father took my chair when he came in here. I'll not give it up again. Not when power matters this much. Not when I'm "Coco with her little shop."

I don't relish being used. The whole thing smacks of me being a fool, which I am not. Beneath the shame of it all, I am angry I fell for it in the first place.

Rome takes his time sitting down, sizing up the desk that

separates us. "First off, Orlando shouldn't have told you that. I didn't want you to know it was me who was behind your rent decrease. I just wanted to do something nice for you. I've opened my fair share of new businesses before. The first year is hard. You're taking a big risk, opening up here. I believe in what you're doing—in the statement of peace you're making. I didn't want the whole thing to fold over something as stupid as money." He holds up his hands. "You weren't supposed to know it was me, so there's no quid pro quo coming. That's how our fathers do things, tré-sur." He holds my gaze with a no-nonsense firmness. "I am not my father."

My retort comes through gritted teeth. "My name is Colette Kennedy. I am not your treasure. I'm your joke."

He holds up his hands, though I can see my firm words skewer him. "Apologies, Miss Kennedy."

I am not ready to give up my indignation, though his argument is doing its best to defuse each of my points. "I see what you're doing, Rome. Orlando laid it all out for me. You're being sweet to me to piss off my family. Maybe that's why you helped out with my rent. I'm not stupid enough to think there's something real between us."

Though I try to sound flippant, the smack of true hurt crackles in the air between us.

Rome stands slowly, pressing his hands on my desk so he can tower over me as he leans forward. "I want you to listen to me now. I don't fall for pretty faces and long legs

—though you've got both of those in spades. What turns my head is a woman who can see me—really see me—and keep up with all I've got going. I'm just as thrown by this whole thing as you are. I want peace between our families just as much as you do."

"Is that what you told Angelica?"

He holds up his finger, pulling out his phone. "I'm not doing this twice. Hold on." When his call connects, he turns his phone on speaker. "Orlando, I'm not dating Angelica. It's Colette I'm interested in. Angelica kissed my cheek, is all, and I made things clear to her that I'm not up for grabs."

My breath stills in my chest. "What are you doing?" I shout-whisper.

Rome holds his finger up to me, waiting for Orlando's reply.

Orlando's voice fills my office. "I know what you're doing, and now Coco does, too. I didn't save her life so you could mess with her head. You're mad at Elias for leaving us high and dry when he didn't come through on his end of the deal after we bought all those patrol cars. You're stringing Coco along so you can stick it to her family. I'll have your back through just about anything, Rome. You know that. But I'm not going to look the other way on this. She's been jerked around enough. She doesn't deserve to pay for what her father did to us."

A lump forms in my throat, grateful to Orlando for this and so many other reasons.

Rome grips the edge of my desk, closing his eyes as if this conversation truly pains him. "I want both of you to listen to me now. I couldn't care less about the patrol cars. Money is no reason to retaliate. Money means nothing. It buys loyalty. When it doesn't, then it's just paper with dead people printed on it. The sheriff took useless paper from me. If I was going to play the angle of seducing his only daughter, I would have sent Nico in for the job."

I scoff at the notion.

Rome meets my eyes across the desk. I can see the fire of hard truth blazing in his blue orbs. "I don't want to stick anything to your dad. When I came by that night it all started, it was to make amends for Nico trashing your salon. I didn't count on falling for you, but that's exactly what happened. Do you think I read poetry to just anyone? Do you know the last time I made cannoli by hand? Do you have any idea how little I want to be with any other woman? It's you, tré-sur. If I wanted to rub your father's nose in it, I would've done that the first day. I wouldn't be still sneaking around, hoping not to get caught because I know that would cause a fight with your family." He presses his finger to the center of my desk. "I have just as much to lose as you do in all of this. But none of that matters to me. Everything I've worked for feels foolish. I want to be with you, Coletta. Only you. Always you."

I have no idea what to make of any of this, even as Orlando groans on the other end. "Are you serious? Why, Rome? Why her? I was mad when I thought you were stringing her along, but this is way worse. Dating a Kennedy is a death sentence. Fintan is mental and the sheriff's not far behind. They keep tabs on everything she does. They try to control each move she makes. One whiff of this, and they'll send her overseas again." I can picture Orlando shaking his head. "You're insane. Absolutely insane. Go be with Angelica if you're lonely. Not a Kennedy."

Rome doesn't acknowledge Orlando at all. He loses a fair amount of his tough demeanor when he reaches across the desk to thumb a tear from my cheek that I didn't realize had fallen. His entire body softens, along with his voice. "There is no one else, tré-sur. Only you. I met with Angelica in a public place because I wanted your rent lowered. I didn't realize she thought we were on a date. The second I did, I got out of there as quick as I could."

My voice comes out just above a whisper. "Why did you do that, if not to keep me in your pocket, owing you a favor for that favor?"

Rome shakes his head at me. "You are too good at living in this city, Coletta. I hate that this place has jaded you so much that you can't fathom someone supporting you without a selfish motive. I want to make your life better. I will not be just another person in your life who uses you. If I can't be with you, I still want you to succeed, even if I have to watch you shine from afar. Anyone who bests me with their bravery deserves that." He pauses, pursing his lips while his nostrils flare. "I am never surprised. But you doing something bold like opening a Kennedy business in Midtown that serves both humans and vampires? No one saw that coming." He jabs his finger to the center of my desk. "I would have helped you regardless because I believe in the truce, and I'm damn impressed with your moxie."

Rome starts pacing, his words turning into somewhat of a rant. "Falling for you was never part of my plan." His tone turns sour, as if he is arguing with me, frustrated with my silence. "I don't have time for a woman I care about. I don't have the energy to stick around and work things out when the road gets muddy. Yet here I am, duking it out with you because I won't be able to sleep tonight if you think I only want you so I can start a war."

He stops pacing and points to the exit. "If I had a lick of sense, I would march out of here right now and never look back. I would write you off as just a nice pair of tits and that's that. But I'm here, making sure you know I am behind you, fighting for your success because I believe in your vision." He motions around the room. "No one believes in Mayfield! The only reason humans move here is for the tax break they get from donating blood on a monthly basis. Then you, with all your smarts and talent come back to this hellhole and breathe life into me just when I was sure this place was going to suffocate my last shred of hope."

He looks distressed, his eyes round with a wild quality to them.

I had no idea he felt any of this. He might be breathless, but I am speechless.

Rome pauses for a breath, quieting marginally. "I honestly like you, Colette. You are not my joke. You're a treasure."

18

FIRST KISS
COLETTE

All the arguments I had stored up leave me feeling foolish for suspecting the worst of Rome.

"I didn't believe in you," comes my hushed reply. "I didn't believe the best but jumped right to the worst." I lower my chin because I can admit when I am wrong, even if it feels like crap. "You tried to help me, and I shanked you for it. I'm sorry, Rome. I got all turned around."

I expect a haughty "No kidding," but instead I get a measured yet firm, "Coletta, I am not leaving this office until I kiss you."

I glance up, certain I heard him wrong. "What?"

Orlando's voice crackles at a higher pitch. "Um, guys? Could you not include me in this? Sorry for the mix-up, Rome. You alright, Coco?"

I nod, sniffling as I swipe the heel of my palm across my cheek. "I think so."

Rome picks up the phone. "You did the right thing, Orlando. Always check my steps to make sure I'm not putting a toe out of line. I don't like that you didn't come to me with this, but anyone who cares about my tré-sur can stab me in the back all he wants if he thinks he is protecting her. You're a good man."

Orlando grumbles. "How about you kiss her and tell me nothing about it. This is officially me knowing nothing about the bomb you two are playing with. This is a bad idea, Cousin. It was bad when I thought you were stringing her along. It's somehow worse now that it's all for real."

Rome ends the call, meeting my gaze with utter sincerity beaming from him.

It's the first time I notice the bags under his eyes, though it's barely noon. "I'm sorry I put you through all of that."

Rome excuses my apology with a wave of his hand. "I think we handled our first fight fairly well." He points to the space between us. "I wasn't kidding, though. I'm not leaving until I kiss you."

I guffaw at his gall. "Are you serious? I'm a mess. I've been crying and I just accused you of... This is hardly a romantic moment."

"Good. Maybe you'll be a terrible kisser. Then I'll be able to kick this infatuation once and for all. I haven't been able to stop thinking about you. It's not like me. I'm acting like a mated man."

I guffaw, baffled at his choice of words. "Well, you're not. Vampires can't mate with humans. That's not a thing."

Rome rolls his eyes at the obvious fact. "I know that. And I know it's not really happening, but from what other vampires have described, this is what that sounds like." He shakes his head, fear suddenly coming over him. "Being mated is a fate worse than death. There are a lot of obvious reasons why we shouldn't be together, but one relief is that we can never be mated."

I tilt my head at him. "Is it really so horrible?" I hold up my hands. "I don't know much about it."

"It's the worst fate I can think of. If it was us, I could feel your lower swings. If you were upset with me, I wouldn't be able to sleep until you were okay. I mean, talk about a recipe for instant manipulation. I wouldn't care as much about Mayfield or my family or even myself. You and your needs would be the center of my universe, whether you were a good person or not. I would be beholden to you."

I swallow hard. "It sounds like love, but with obsession added in. You're right; that does sound bad."

"I'm glad we won't have to deal with that. We can dote on each other in a healthy, normal way." His mouth pulls to the side. "Like, you know, sneaking around so no one finds out about us."

I snigger.

Rome runs his hand through his hair. "I like knowing

that my feelings are mine. That some magical force isn't controlling me. I don't mind that I can't stop thinking about you. I keep going out of my way to make sure your life is better because it's *my* choice. I'm falling faster than I thought possible. Sometimes it scares me." His nose crinkles in disgust. "I don't make cannoli for people!"

I blink up at him, uncertain of so much, but unwilling to leave before I understand. "That's a shame. It was delicious."

"You ate them?"

"I ate part of one." My voice lowers as if I am confessing to a crime. "It was the best dessert of my life. You should make them more often, Rome."

"I guess I'll be making them more often." The corner of his mouth lifts. I am fairly certain Rome has never been sexier. Then a plea comes over him, almost as if the small gap between our bodies is causing him physical pain. "Please, Coletta."

Kissing Rome isn't a line I should be crossing, but when I stand, I know that is exactly what I am about to do. "One kiss, and maybe the crush will fade. You're right. Maybe you taste like blood and dirty fish."

He moves around my desk to stand in front of me, blanching at my description. "Best get this out of our system. It's nothing more than old-fashioned infatuation. Scratch the itch, and it goes away."

Though as he says the words, it's clear neither of us believes them.

"Don't go away," he whispers, sounding very much like a man with his heart on his sleeve.

I can't believe I questioned him.

When he reaches out to touch my face, I bite down on my lower lip. I love the feel of his fingers on my cheek, tracing my top lip as if he has no idea what that does to a woman. We have talked on the phone every night since our big encounter, and I have imagined him doing exactly this every time.

"Stop me," he warns. "I shouldn't be kissing you."

"Rome," I breathe, wondering if he can hear the uneven hammering of my heart.

When his lips touch on mine, the entire world stops spinning. The bustle of the salon on the other side of my door fades into nothing when his lips connect with mine so very tenderly.

This isn't happening. I've imagined this dozens of times since that first night when he came to the salon, but the anticipation of this scandal is nothing to the reality of this moment. It's not the forbidden nature of our pairing (though that's in the mix, to be sure); it's the softness of Rome's lips that instantly addicts me to the act of kissing this beautiful man.

Both of us freeze while the world cracks in two and shatters around us, bowing to the newness of our kiss.

Rome's thumb sweeps over the apple of my cheek, and I'm a goner. My lips part for another, and then another. Soon enough, I am collecting kisses like perfect petals sent from above just for me. Rome tastes like a cinnamon treat that I cannot stop savoring. His lips are soft with their cunning tease. They might never stop drawing me in, now that I've had my first taste.

I was supposed to kick my crush, not run headfirst into the euphoria. But the more I taste of Rome's lips, the headier my obsession becomes. His kiss morphs from hesitant and uncertain to firm and fulfilling. He cusses between kisses now, holding my face so he can lean into the passion. "This wasn't supposed to happen."

My hand reaches up, taking on a life of its own so it can fulfill its fantasy of feeling the firmness of his pecs. "We should stop." But we both know I won't. I don't think I could pull away if I wanted to, which I don't.

If anything, I need more.

I tug him closer, biting down on the freckle dotting his lower lip. I haven't been able to scrub it from my mind, so I take it between my lips, claiming it as my treasure.

His moan of desire floods my senses, overriding the common sense that would have me hold back from what I want.

I hate that my life has been about holding back, that I have to question my desire this much. I am expected to settle for ice cold blind dates. What I really want is the heat that Rome and I can conjure out of hope and a fight right here in my office.

I can feel his fangs, which is a new thrill that comes from doing something dangerous. All vampires have more pronounced canines, though nothing terribly dramatic or animalistic. Still, I notice the difference when my tongue dances with his, sweeping across his top row of teeth just because I can.

"Am I scaring you?" Rome asks, sounding genuinely worried. Like if there was a way he could hide his canines from me, he would.

"No," I tell him between kisses. "I'm safe with you." And it really is true. I'm not afraid he'll bite me. I am the one person in the world who is protected from that fate. Because if Rome bit me once, he would die on the spot.

Yes, it's a dangerous game we're playing, toying with fate, which so clearly wants us to be far apart.

"You *are* safe with me," Rome promises, and I truly believe him.

His free arm wraps around me, pressing my body to his so there is no escaping the harsh reality that this is happening. Neither of us are going to pull the cord to stop this thing. Desperation takes over both of us at the exact same moment, turning the passionate kiss into rough grabbing and messy kisses that grow more chaotic by the second. My chair is pushed away from us and papers scatter to the floor.

He doesn't go easy on me, and I love the ride.

I fight back just as hard, kissing and biting while his groans trade themselves for mine, filling the air with a desperation I never want to give up. I don't want something safer if it means forfeiting the feel of his hands on me. He grabs onto my hip, coveting the spot he told me he has been lusting after.

My body arcs for him, giving itself over so he can play and peruse while I explore his tight torso. I want to see his chest. I want to kiss a line down his sternum. Heat flares in me so much that my fingers do what they want before my brain can decide if this is a good idea.

The more I have of Rome, the more I want.

As I unbutton and untuck his shirt, I am well aware we passed reason a long time ago. There is no common sense, only craving as I tear his shirt down his arms, kissing him hard enough to stave off any resistance that threatens to separate us. His undershirt slides over his head, giving me the view I have been salivating for.

I need this man, this kiss, and I normally don't like needing anything I can't do myself. But there is no question about it: the more I have of Rome, the more I *must* have. My palms slide over the musculature of his chest, addicting me further.

The air shifts around us, sending a chill through my body—a warning of something to come.

I'm not sure if I hear it or I feel it, but a clear and

distinct popping vibration sends a jolt from my palms into his chest, surprising us both.

Did I give him a static shock?

"Something's happening," Rome tells me. He rubs his chest but then fuses his lips to mine again, as if he needs to be kissing me to breathe properly.

I very much know the feeling.

"Coletta?" He sounds worried, yet his kisses are certain, determined we will make the most of this stolen moment. "Did you feel that?"

The reality of the danger we are steeped in floods me like a warning shot from a gun, finally breaking me away from him. It's as if my conscience shoved me back. "Rome, be careful! We have to stop. Did I hurt you?" I touch my lip, suddenly terrified. "If you nick my lip with your fangs, you'll die!"

And just like that, I am on the other side of the office, clinging to the wall, not because he is the danger, but because *I* am. I could have killed him. I wasn't exactly careful, losing all control like that.

Rome's undershirt slides back over his torso, but his dress shirt is hanging open as he presses his hand to his heart. His breath comes in rough gusts while he struggles to get ahold of himself. "It's okay. I'm okay. It's not your blood; it's something else." He touches his heart. "I feel strange. Did you feel that? Something popping?"

I nod, overwhelmed and on the edge of a breakdown. "Tell me I didn't hurt you!"

Rome's entire demeanor softens as he clears the gap between us, holding my face in his hands. "You didn't hurt me, tré-sur. I don't know what that was. Like something cut my chest, but there's no mark. I'm not even sure it was painful, only surprising. Are you okay?"

I gape up at him, flustered and completely at a loss. My voice comes out shrill and pinched. "Are you kidding me? None of what we just did is okay! I could have killed you! You realize that, yes? My blood is dangerous for you to be near. I'm... Rome, I'm so sorry! I lost my head. I wasn't thinking."

"You were feeling?" Rome thumbs my cheekbones, peering into my face with compassion and genuine concern for my angst. There's not a trace of fear for his own life. "I know what you mean. I can't remember the last time I let go and actually enjoyed a moment. That was incredible." He kisses my lips just once, soft and gentle—a tender offering of sweetness to smooth over the ravaging we did to each other. "Everything is fine. We'll take this slower, so you don't worry about anything bad happening when we kiss."

Then Rome does something so precious, my knees actually go weak. He nuzzles my nose, moving from left to right. I quiver through the shockwaves his sweetness sends through my entire being.

I savor the loveliness, holding it in my heart so I can remember this beautiful moment for years to come. Everything about him is brighter now, less encumbered by life.

When a knock stiffens my spine, Rome pecks my lips. "I'll handle it. Everything is going to be fine. Say it, Coletta."

"Everything is going to be fine," I echo, though we both know it's not.

When Rome pulls away from me to button up his shirt and open the door, my body immediately feels the absence. "Just finishing up. Your boss will be out in a minute."

Rachel's voice is tight but cheerful. "Can you tell her we're running low on her shampoo?"

"Will do."

The moment Rome shuts the door and locks it behind him, I bury my face in my hands. "She knows! This is going to be a disaster, Rome."

I'm surprised to find strong arms around me. "She doesn't suspect a thing. It's alright."

Being held is somehow just as impactful as our earth-shattering kiss. I cannot remember the last time a man wrapped his arms around me so beautifully. Being treated like a uterus to be auctioned off has made me wary of men. Whenever I've needed to be held, I held myself, or I hugged Declan. There weren't many men willing to wrap their arms around me who didn't have some serious agenda behind the show of sweetness.

Yet as Rome holds me to his chest, gently rocking me from side to side, I realize more fully the bliss I have been missing out on all these years. My worries aren't all on me to figure out by myself anymore; he is bearing a few of them so I'm not in this alone.

I never want him to let me go.

"This," I tell him, closing my eyes while my heart flutters against his. "I need more of this. Always this." I could burrow my body in his embrace and never feel the need to shake off the closeness.

"I will not let anything bad happen to us," Rome promises, though I know there is no way he can make good on that. "Now we know this isn't just a crush. Let's not waste any more time pretending this is something that will fade away. I want to be with you, Coletta, whatever that looks like."

Panic threatens to rise in me again. "It's not possible!"

"What's not possible is pretending we can go our separate ways." Rome tilts my chin up so he can kiss me again, reminding us both of the beauty that is worth fighting for. "I will find a way." His eyes grow serious as he searches my face. "Which day can you slip away each week?"

I shake my head. "The family is everywhere. I take one day off a week, and I use it to run errands."

"You might need to run errands in Fowlerville."

I balk at his suggestion, but then start to see his reasoning. "No one from the city is driving three hours away on a Wednesday. You're right."

"Wednesdays, it is. I'll meet you at..." He pauses, and I can tell he's fishing around for a landmark. "There's a beach in Fowlerville. I'll meet you there at noon, and we'll spend the day together. Promise me, Coletta. I won't let you slip through my fingers. My assistant will run your errands. I need that day with you."

I swallow hard, knowing this has gone well beyond anything I can put a stop to now. I've already crossed a line by kissing him, but this? We're making plans together.

I should end it now, but when I open my mouth, I know I cannot be untrue to myself and still sleep at night. "It's a date."

Pure joy sweeps over Rome, lighting up his entire body.

I've never seen his full-blown smile before. The sight of something this magnificent takes me by surprise. My mouth falls open in wonder, gaping up at the sight that is Rome when he is truly happy. I can't stop staring; I am utterly transfixed. "You're beautiful," I gasp, giving in to unvarnished honesty, since that is the game we're playing.

He chuckles lightly, kissing me once more and squeezing me close.

The steady beat of his heart lulls me. It's louder than it should be, or maybe I am more attuned to him because he is pressed up against me. But even when he releases my body so he can tuck in his shirt and reassemble himself, his heartbeat remains in my ears.

And that's when it hits me that I belong in Rome's arms, cuddled close. The thrum of his heart is now louder to me than the disapproving noise of the rest of the world.

19

PICNIC PREP
ROME

I have been awake since yesterday morning. I can't stop planning our time together in my mind, going over the details et nauseum to make sure I have covered my bases. It's ridiculous, of course. We're going to a beach three hours away from the city. No one will see us there.

Even if passersby did, would they know something was off? Vampires blend in seamlessly because we look like normal humans. Sure, we heal faster and our hankering for blood is no secret, but other than those hiccups, we're not that much different from the rest of the population. Just because we have been herded to all live in the West End of Mayfield doesn't mean that we haven't assimilated into the population on occasion.

It was the quickest way to get property values to plummet, to be sure. Once a vampire moved in, everyone else moved out. It became hard to find a realtor to sell to our kind. Mama Kennedy used to be our realtor. She made it a point to sell only to vampires, giving us options outside of Mayfield's West End.

Of course, her dream for us to live in proper society died when she passed. Vampires were corralled to the West End of Mayfield—the only place where we are now allowed to live.

The humans have us where they want us, so they feel safer.

Good for them. Meanwhile our schools are underfunded and the tax money we pay seems to go to anything but beautifying our side of the city.

But none of that matters today. Not too many people frequent the beach in the middle of a workday in the early fall. Kids will be in school, and most won't bother swimming when the weather isn't balmy. Colette and I will have the whole beach to ourselves.

She is a recognizable face, as am I, so finding a private spot to be together is tricky, but important.

I don't need to leave for another half an hour, but after trying to fill my time cramming in a hundred sit-ups so I don't look old in front of Colette in a bathing suit, I realize I am driving myself crazy.

I want her so badly. I need to sweep away all the reasons that might pop into her mind that might try to convince her I am not worth the risk.

I know myself, so I am certain that she is it for me.

When I meander into my spacious kitchen, I pull out the travel cooler from the doublewide stainless-steel fridge and set it on the marble countertop. I packed our picnic lunch when I was supposed to be sleeping, but was too fidgety to rest.

Orlando's footsteps are hard to miss; he's the largest in the family and has a sixth sense when I am unsettled. "Morning, cousin. What are..." When his gaze hits the cooler, his mouth firms. "Are we talking about what a bad idea it is to hook up with the Kennedy girl?"

I raise my chin and keep my gaze from his scrutiny. "Nope. I'm not talking about any of it, actually. I'm taking a day off."

Orlando scoffs, as if I've cracked a joke. "That's funny. What are you really doing?"

I pop open the cooler to show him the sandwiches, tapenade, crackers, wine and raspberry cannoli.

That's right. I know my girl's vices.

Orlando's nose scrunches. "I don't get it."

I roll my eyes at the both of us, because if he came to me with a fancy lunch packed like this, I would think he had similarly lost his mind. "It's a picnic. This is what normal people do when they are dating. I'm meeting up with Colette out of town so we can actually give this thing a go. There are too many eyes in the city."

Orlando's movements are stiff as he pours himself some coffee. "There are eyes everywhere! You get that, right? Colette is a recognizable figure, being the Last Deadblood. And you're a public persona, too, Rome. Everyone knows you run the West End. You're the most influential vampire there is. When humans think the word 'vampire,' it's your face they see." Orlando shakes his head as he blows on his hot cup. "This is a bad idea. I don't understand your game. Are you trying to piss off the sheriff? Are you trying to stick it to Fintan? Because all of that should be beneath you."

My teeth grind, but it's not Orlando's fault. These are fair questions. A month ago, I might be asking the same thing if it was Nico in my position.

"I'm trying to date a woman. That's all. It's nothing more complicated or seedy than that. We're going out of town, so we don't run into her family. Hopefully, people will leave us alone so we can enjoy our lives for a single day."

Perhaps that's a touch too much melodrama. But that doesn't stop it from being true.

I tuck silverware, plates and napkins into the cooler. "Maybe if we're out together, like a normal couple, I can shake her out of my system." Though, even as I say this, there's a foul taste in my mouth. I don't want Colette out of my system. I want her in my arms. I want to suck on her lower lip and bury my face in her neck.

I want to nip at her hip and trace the curve of her side with my tongue.

Hunger rises in my body, reminding me of all the nuances she has that I haven't been able to shake from my memory. She touches her thumb to each of her fingers in order when she is anxious, and then starts over until she says her piece.

She wears heels at a job where she's on her feet all day.

Her lips are dark pink, and every now and then, she presses them together when she doesn't like what I say. That simple tease tempts me to utter all sort of ungentlemanly things just so I can watch her disapprove of my antics.

Orlando motions to me with a finger. "You need to feed before you go."

"I fed yesterday. You were there." I know I sound petulant, but I don't like being told things a basic five-year-old vampire understands. We have to drink about a pint of blood every week, or we'll start to get thirsty. Thirst leads to irrational situations, like a vampire trying to feed on a stranger instead of going to the blood bank for donated blood, like a civilized vampire should.

"Yeah, but you're going to be spending time alone with the one woman who could kill you if you get thirsty and forget yourself."

I twist my ring on my finger, examining the family crest.

As much as my father adored Coletta, I know he would not approve of what I am doing.

I narrow my eyes at my cousin. "I haven't been thirsty in years. I'm an adult, Orlando." Drinking once a week means I don't feel the pangs of thirst at all, so I can live a relatively normal life.

"Really? Because you're sneaking around like a teenager." He leans his elbows on the counter. "You do realize we babysat her, right? Our differing races aside, you're ten years older than she is. That's weird."

I don't address his last point because it's not one I can argue my way out of. I've slowly allowed myself to become obsessed with the worry that I might look old to her, so I've been overdoing it with pushups and sit-ups to compensate.

I pull a blood bag from the fridge and pop the tab, sticking a straw in through the hole. Hopefully this satisfies Orlando's worry that I might be thirsty, even though I am a grown man who knows the basics of how to tie my shoes.

I drain half the bag and put the rest in the fridge. "There. Satisfied?"

Orlando sips his coffee, which has to be too hot to drink yet. "Overjoyed. You want me to check on Martin's Dry Cleaning today?"

Thank goodness he switches his focus toward work. "That's a good place to start. Their numbers are too low for them to be laundering money through the business, but there have been a fair few shady people getting their clothes dry cleaned for everything to be aboveboard. I know Martin is selling halluci-blend. I just don't have the proof."

Orlando sips his coffee. "I'm on your side. I'll get another look at their books if you like."

I shake my head. "No. They'll just show us the same fabrication they handed us before. We're missing something. I can feel it."

"They're not cooking drugs in the laundromat. We did a thorough search. The sheriff searched them, too. There's only so much we can do with a hunch, Rome." Orlando pauses to let his words settle in the air. My cousin thinks my hunch is wrong, but he is being diplomatic about it. "Sooner or later, we have to admit that the problem might not be coming from the laundromat."

I know it's Orlando's job to question me and make me think things through, but I know when I am on the right track, and this is one of those times.

"I'm taking the copy of their books with me in case I beat Colette there. I'll give them another look. I'm missing something; I can feel it. This is the spot the halluci-blend is coming from."

I finish packing the cooler and load it into my car, along with a bathing suit and two towels, a picnic blanket, and the copy of the laundromat's financials.

Orlando doesn't say anything more as he drinks his

coffee and watches me pack the car. He doesn't laugh when I look up on my phone a list of things one might need to create the perfect romantic picnic.

I will never live this down if my search history is made public.

Orlando doesn't have a hint of teasing to him when I leave for the day. But I know what my cousin is thinking.

This is a mistake. Coletta and I are a dangerous mistake.

The problem is that I agree with him...

...I just don't care.

20

SWIMMING

COLETTE

I am careful the entire way not to go over the speed limit, worried more than usual that I might get pulled over. Though I have never had a ticket in my life (thanks to my father being who he is, coupled with my diplomatic immunity that pretty much gets me out of every jam), I still concern myself with being a rule follower. I break only the rules that are in desperate need of shattering.

I turned around twice on the way here, so I arrive later than I told Rome I would be. He hasn't texted me to ask where I am at, and I'm too chicken to call him and tell him I am scared to meet. If we go on this date—this day away from everyone who feels permission to dictate the particulars of my love life—it will be official. Right now, it's still a clandestine affair—me cheating on my own people.

My fingers are shaking. That's not a good sign. If I don't

get my nerves under control, I won't be able to go at all. I don't want my stupid condition to be the reason I don't show up. I want to be the one who makes the call, not my failing health.

I take my pill with a snarl. I've been trying to ween myself off them, but on days like this, it's not an option. Anxiety makes my tremors worse. I don't want to get there and be such a wreck that I have to admit to Rome how sick I really am.

No, he doesn't need to know about that. First dates are supposed to be about fun and flirtation.

Though, I am not sure either of us are the type to commit to those things without taking in the ramifications such levities could cause.

I am sweating because this is insanity. Even as I pull into the almost empty parking lot of the beach, I'm still unsure if I should get out of the car. My hands are steady again, thank goodness, but my heart is a series of nervous pitters and patters.

I'm not supposed to get worked up.

Well, if we're making a list of the things I'm not supposed to do, moving back to Mayfield, away from my doctor is number one.

Number two is opening a branch of my business with stakes this high. So really, meeting Rome for a date isn't even at the top of the activities my doctor would throw a fit about.

I don't know why that doesn't make me more confident. As it is, I am fairly certain I just drove three hours only to be half an hour late to a date I might bail on. I want Rome too badly. I can't objectively look at our pairing and see it for the bad idea it obviously is.

Rome will understand. If I drive home right now and don't tell him a thing, he will surmise it was too much for me. It's too much for any human, really. I've never heard of a human hooking up with a vampire, much less going on a proper date with one. We preach tolerance but not acceptance of the other race. Tolerance and acceptance are two very different things. Our family was a big pioneer back in the day, making it a point to go places together with the Valentinos. We went on family vacations, worked and studied together.

And here I am, grown into an adult who cannot decide whose opinion matters more—my own or a slew of strangers, plus a brother and a father whom I don't respect to begin with.

I should tell Declan, though.

I should, but I know I won't.

My shoulders slump as my forehead leans on the steering wheel.

I am pathetic. My mother would be ashamed of me for treating a member of the Valentino family like this.

Then again, I'm sure when Rome and Fintan occasionally had to watch over Nino-bear and me, she wasn't exactly hoping her little girl would hook up with her babysitter.

Yep. This is too weird. I reach for the keys to shove them into the ignition, but just as I do, my eyes fall on Rome. He is leaning against a tree to the left of where I've parked, hands in his pockets.

I wonder how long he's been staring at me, watching my existential crisis play out and land far from his favor.

I should leave. He would understand if I pealed out right now with no explanation. But even with the distance dividing us, I cannot bring myself to back away from the magnetic pull he seems to have on me lately.

He doesn't move toward me, trying (and failing) to project a cool demeanor. It clashes with his laser focus on me when I finally open my car door. I don't often wear flipflops, cutoffs and a tight pink t-shirt, but I am definitely dressed for flirting at the beach today.

I never did that when I lived overseas. Once I got on my feet, I was too busy studying and working to bother with dating. Plus, the only people who tried to date me made it crystal clear that they only wanted me for my place in the revolution, wherein the goal would be to extinguish all vampires using my blood as their weapon.

How romantic.

My steps are careful as I walk toward Rome with my towel over my arm. "I'm late," I admit in lieu of a greeting. I stop a few feet from him, pursing my lips because I'm not sure how to proceed.

"You showed up," he counters, not holding me accountable for my rudeness. "I'm glad."

"Really? Because you look stressed." I motion to his tensed neck muscles.

Rome shrugs. "You don't think I fit in at a beach setting? You can't picture me swimming and tanning and all that?"

The corner of my mouth quirks, but then the levity falls. "I turned around three times on the way here."

He nods once, taking in the information without giving me a hint of how he is processing it.

Darn his beautiful poker face.

When he doesn't speak, I start rambling like an idiot. "I'm nervous. This is... you know how big of a deal it is that we're sneaking around. Phone calls were one thing, but this is a big step. If my family found out, it would be bad. I don't know that a few kisses are worth the drama that's going to rain down on your head if this thing blows in the wrong direction."

He keeps his hands in his pockets, studying my movements. He remains silent, which I know from watching our fathers in action is an interrogation technique. It works easily on a guilty conscience.

"But maybe this is more than a few kisses." My cheeks pink as soon as the words come out of my mouth. "Not like that. Not like sex." I cringe at how stupid I sound. "I mean all of it. A relationship. If they find out there are feelings involved, it's not going to go over well. I try to pick and choose how many heart attacks I give my father. Opening up a business in Midtown is enough for him to worry about. Adding a vampire boyfriend into the mix?" My eyes widen. "Not that you're my boyfriend. We haven't even talked about that. I'm not assuming..." I pause to pinch the bridge of my nose, cursing myself for not staying home this morning.

Rome doesn't speak. He only holds out his hand in silent invitation.

Darn him for doing the perfect thing.

My heart hammers as I stumble toward him like a newborn fawn. I don't hold onto his fingers but drop my towel on the grass so I can throw my arms around his neck. "I'm sorry," I whisper. "I shouldn't have kept you waiting. I'm scared, and I'm not sure that'll go away anytime soon."

His arms curve easily around my waist. My torso pressed to his feels like the most natural thing in the world. "Are you scared of me, Colette?"

I shake my head as my fingers tangle in his freshly cut hair. "No. I'm scared of *us*."

His cheek presses to mine, not judging my fear or trying to brush it aside. His lips tickle the shell of my ear. His reply is more soothing than a lullaby. "Then we'll take this slow."

"Stop saying the perfect thing. It only makes me want you more."

He thumbs at the small of my back, warming my body at the simple touch. My hips marry to his as I lean up on my toes. That little tease of a touch at the base of my spine leeches a flood of anxiety out of me. There's protection in that touch—a shelter the wind cannot tear apart. His body curves around mine so I can finally begin to exhale in his arms.

My body trusts him, even if my brain is unsure.

We stand there like that, with my arms around his neck and my cheek pressed to his. I'm certain he will let me remain in his arms for as long as I need. He anchors me to this spot so I don't fly away home, back where it's safer and life is predictable. His thumb unties the strings that have me tightly wound. He takes his time toying with the few inches at the base of my spine, sweeping across the bare skin as if we were never meant to hide secrets from each other.

My heels finally hit the grass and my palm slides from his shoulder to his chest. My thumb traces his musculature from side to side, examining the hard feel of one pectoral compared to the other.

I love this spot on his body. It calls to me every time he comes near.

"Mm." The low contented sound rumbles in his chest, reminding me that he is very much a man, and I am pressed up against him like I've never heard the words "we'll take this slow." I angle my chin up because I need to feel his breath on my face. I want to bathe in the masculine scent of him.

I can't not kiss this beautiful man. Not when he's looking at me like that.

Like I could never offend him.

Like my worries are all that matter to him.

I know it's not true. He's got the world on his shoulders —or at least his third of Mayfield is on his shoulders, which is the entire vampire population of the world. Still, he pauses all of that and drinks in my features as if I captivate his attention no matter which storm he's mired in.

His lips are soft when they meet mine. Before Rome, I hadn't been kissed in years. I was so out of practice, I worried I'd forgotten how. But this beautiful man is patient with my imperfections. He keeps one hand on the base of my spine while the other traces the apple of my cheek, turning my face to just the right angle for him to do as he pleases.

Oh, how he pleases me. One kiss multiplies quickly, trailing into a whole field of bliss. I don't remember it being like this when I kissed other guys. Maybe there's a difference between making out with a guy and kissing a real man. Maybe it's the added scandal of our differing races coming into play. Whatever it is, I can't get enough. I want miles and miles of this. The more he kisses me, the further away my worries about our date become, until they are so far in the distance, I can't be bothered by them any longer.

"Only me," he murmurs between kisses. "Tell me you'll only kiss me."

"Only you." It's an easy promise to make.

This isn't exactly slow, swearing exclusivity on our first date, but I don't care. Kissing another man would be a punishment, now that I've been spoiled by Rome's sensual lips.

He presses his mouth harder to mine, reminding me of his fangs. The added edge of danger could be a thrill, but it's a true testament to the fact that I actually care about this man when I back off, tapering the kiss with pitters and patters of affection instead of an all-out plundering. One nick of his fangs on my lips, and he could die right in front of me.

This fire we're playing with could burn us both if we're not careful.

Rome's lashes flutter contentedly as he holds me to him. "Mm."

I love that delicious noise he makes, letting me know I am having just as much an effect on him as he is having on me.

Now that I am here in his arms, I know I will never want to be anywhere else.

Yes, this is going to get messy.

21

ONLY YOU

COLETTE

Rome thumbs the curve of my hip as the lake air teases my thick curls. "This is a good beach. I like it here."

Though, he's not looking at the lake, but at me.

I rub his chest and rest my cheek against his shoulder. "I like it here, too." I love the way his chuckle vibrates through the solid structure of his chest. "Do you want to go for a swim?"

Rome hesitates before he answers. "I suggested the beach because it's far away, but I almost couldn't find my bathing suit. It hasn't been used in like, a decade. Probably not since our families went to the lake together on joint vacations."

His stomach tightens with a grimace. I know it's because he feels old and didn't mean to give voice to it.

I bury a kiss in the side of his neck. "Let's give it a shot.

But first, how about we stay here like this for a little longer." My voice is quiet, as if I am unaccustomed to asking for what I want.

Perhaps the quaver in my voice is because what I want isn't something I should be voicing at all.

"We can stay like this forever." Rome's answer is simple, but I can tell it surprises him as thoroughly as it does me. As much as my picky brain wants to convince me he makes declarations like this all the time to women, I can tell that's not the case. He's a private person, just like me.

I guess we're both entering a whole new world with this.

Rome is my indulgence, my delicious treat that I don't have to put down after a few nibbles.

He holds me while he leans his back against the tree. His arms curve around me because our bodies can agree that there is nothing better in life than this. My lashes flutter shut when he rests his cheek atop my head, holding me in place so I can enjoy this moment. It almost didn't happen because of my own cowardice.

When I am finally ready to part my cheek from his chest, my fingers sift through his to make sure we don't drift away from each other. "Are you ready for a swim? I haven't been in the water since I moved back."

I've been so nervous about the scandal of seeing Rome that I forgot how much I love the beach. A day with no daunting agenda stretches out before us, reminding me that life isn't just for the tackling; it's for living, as well.

"I've got my swimsuit in the car," Rome says, motioning to the only other vehicle in the lot.

It's a little chilly for a swim, sure, but I don't care. It's our one chance to be a normal couple. However thin the charade, I decide I desperately want it today.

"Perfect. I'll meet you in the water." I step away from him toward the waves, which are larger than I am used to. My shirt and shorts come off as soon as my bare feet hit the sand. My sandals dangle between my fingers as a chill rolls through me. I remind myself that this is the fun I missed out on when I was stuck in a physical rehabilitation loop. This is life throwing me a bone and showing me that my best days are stretched out before me.

This wasn't possible for me eight years ago. I could barely make it up the stairs without assistance.

Not anymore. I'm normal now. I wear heels like a diva. I cut people's hair with no hint of trembling anywhere in the air.

The water is pure ice when I run into it. I am fearless because this is my time to live without limits. I swallow my scream as I dive under the water, relishing the tightening of my muscles because again, that's normal.

My arms cut through the water so I can go as deep as I like. I know I shouldn't wander past where I can touch, but I don't care. Today of all days, the rules don't apply. Sure, I can swim, but I'm not supposed to put myself in a situation where I have to rely on muscular control for survival.

I haven't had a true flareup in a year. My medication keeps all of that from ruining my life. I decide to trust it and swim deeper out into the water. I cannot see the other side of the lake, which makes it feel like I am in an ocean, swimming toward a blissful nothing.

If I could run away from my problems this easily, I would do it in a heartbeat. I'm grinning from ear to ear as I swim further and further toward my freedom.

They said I would never be able to live on my own. The doctor said I would have to have full-time help forever.

Screw them all. They don't know what a determined brat I can be when I really want something.

I swim until my arms ache with the effort. Then I turn and tread water, surprised at how far I've gone from the shore.

Rome is standing on the sand, unwilling to set foot in the water. I can't say I blame him. It's still freezing, even several minutes after I immersed myself.

I have to see what he looks like in a bathing suit. I have vague memories of our family going swimming with the Valentinos. Nino-bear and I made sandcastles and played near the shore while Declan swam with Orlando and Fintan in the deeper water. Rome was usually on the shore, watching us all like the consummate grownup he's always been. Even our parents occasionally went into the water, but I don't remember Rome ever coming in more than getting his feet wet.

Once or twice on every trip, I always tried to kick my way out to where Declan, Orlando and Fintan were swimming. I wanted more adventure, smiling at the danger.

As I swim toward the shore, my smile fades at the worry on Rome's face. He's got his arms crossed over his chest as he frowns at the waves. I want to address his displeasure, but the sight of Rome in fitted swim trunks makes me forget anything above the waist.

Of course he's got a sculpted body. That's no surprise. But when I think the term "swim trunks" I picture baggy board shorts that hide the better aspects of a man's lower half.

The suit he's wearing is wine-colored and fitted to his tight backside. They're cut like boxer briefs, only shorter and more tailored.

If I thought I understood true sexiness before, I had no idea what lust actually felt like until the sight of Rome in his butt-sculpting swim shorts did me in.

When I get close enough for my feet to touch the sand, relief pings in the back of my mind. *Safe,* it tells me, sounding like my nurse. I itch to go back out to the deeper water, but the lure of this beautiful man so scantily clad takes precedence above all else.

"You coming in?" I call above the crash of the waves. I love the feel of being buoyant.

"Not unless you're drowning. It's freezing! I don't know what I was thinking, suggesting a beach when fall is just around the corner."

"You were thinking you wanted to show me how sexy you are in those shorts," I call, not holding back my obvious lust. "I'm not sure I've ever seen you wear a color before."

He looks down, arms still crossed, and then tilts his head at me. "I was changing when you got in, so I didn't even get to see your suit."

"Shame." I smirk wickedly at him. "It's barely a suit. A few scraps of material held on by a string." That's not entirely true, but he doesn't need to know that. He needs to get in the water so he can experience the magic of the lake.

Rome swears, running his hand over his mouth. "Come here and show me."

I turn my chin from side to side, mischievous and ready to insist I get my way. I crook my finger in his direction, beckoning him to join me.

"Are you hungry? I brought a picnic lunch."

My heart melts at the thoughtfulness. "You did? That's so sweet. After we swim, yes. I'll be ravenous."

"Is it warmer out where it's deeper?"

Nope. "Sure. Let me warm you up."

He sticks a toe in, looking like a giant baby. He flinches. "It's freezing!"

"Come on in, and I'll let you warm me up however you

like." It's a bold statement, but I trust him. That, and my overactive teenaged hormones aren't enjoying the distance between my half-naked body and his.

That seems to be the ticket. Rome sucks in a lungful of air, steeling himself as he grits his teeth and runs for me.

I laugh at his pained shouts that sound like he is being electrocuted. He doesn't stop when he reaches me but splashes the water with his choppy movements. His arms crash around my waist. He tackles me under the water, giving me a fresh reminder that no, the water doesn't warm up this time of year just because you're in it longer.

When our heads break the surface, Rome's teeth are chattering so bad, there's no chance we'll be kissing anytime soon.

Laughter bubbles out of me as he swears over and over, frozen in place with fists clenched. His body refuses to get used to the cold.

I laugh at his wet features. "Ho! Oh, baby. You look chilly."

He narrows his eyes at me while my laughter grows. I can't stop the happy sound even as I wrap my arms around his neck. I press a kiss to his immovable scowl. To sweeten the deal, my legs twine around his waist, trapping him against me. This is exactly where I want him when he is so scantily clad.

"I'm freezing! This is awful! You look so happy and natural in the water, and I'm an old man wanting my orthopedic mattress and an electric blanket." He swears again. "Is it possible the water's gotten colder?"

I can't stop laughing. I can't help it; I love this version of him when he has an actual reaction to his surroundings. He's so controlled all the time with Orlando and his people. Only I get to see Rome all fidgety and grumpy like this.

"This is it. This is our place. I want to come here every week, even when it's the dead of winter. I want to see you exactly as cute as you are right now."

He scowls at me. "Cute is for teddy bears and puppies. I'm a man and I don't like being cold."

"Then I'm proud of you for pushing yourself and trying something outside of your comfort zone." I kiss his frown again, unable to get my giggles under control. "My precious puppy-wuppy."

He ceases all movement (aside from the shivering he cannot control), meeting my eyes with genuine surprise. "You want to do this again?"

"Exactly this with exactly you." I peck his closed lips.

"We're making plans to date regularly?" Finally a smile sneaks over his demeanor. "I like that." He motions to the waves. "This, I hate. Actual hate. But knowing I get to look forward to Wednesdays every week now is the perfect anti-dote to my dreary workload." He kisses me slowly, letting me taste the luscious smoothness of his lips. I can tell he's mindful of his teeth chattering, so it's a quick slip of his lips against mine. Our foreheads press together, creating a cocoon of intimacy for our secrets. "Thank you. I was worried when you didn't show. I wouldn't have been mad; it's a big deal, what we're doing here. I would have understood if you'd stood me up."

I know he is telling the truth. Rome, of all people, understands how high tempers can fly between our families. It's a big risk we're taking, but it's the only option that makes sense to me.

"I belong where I put myself," I tell him, clinging to my mantra as my body bobs around his. "And in your arms is where I want to be."

Rome kisses me. It's a closed-mouth blessing because his teeth are still chattering too wildly to be safe. When his forehead glues to mine, I can tell by his steadying breaths that he is gearing up to confess something important.

My fingers tangle in his hair at the back of his head, coaxing the truth out because I want to know him.

Rome touches his nose to mine. "I have to warn you, I'm hard to tolerate. That's why I haven't had a steady girlfriend I've been able to commit to for any substantial amount of time. I work a lot."

I can't hold back my amusement. "I had no idea."

A wry smile cracks his face, but then vanishes. "I usually don't like things exclusive, but I know if another man looks at you twice, I won't handle it well. The other women I've dated could come and go, but you?" He shakes his head. "Mine only. And I'll make you the same promise. Yours only."

I chew on my lower lip while I mull over his demands. "I have Friday night obligations once a month. Unless we're willing to tell my family, I have to go on whatever dates Fintan sets up for me. It's one of the reasons they agreed to let me move home."

Rome swallows hard and then nods. "I can understand that. Only first dates, right?"

"Only first dates. My lips and my heart are yours." I don't mean to say that last part, but that doesn't make it any less true. I cannot fathom kissing a man who is not Rome.

But I also cannot fathom telling my brothers and my father that I'm off the market because I want to go to the beach every week with the head of the Valentino family.

"Say it again," Rome demands, his eyes shut tight as if the thought of me dating around causes him actual physical pain.

"I'm yours. Only yours."

He nods a few times, no doubt committing my promise to memory so he can call upon it when I have to go out on the forced blind dates.

Rome kisses me again. "I'm overbearing when I care about something or someone. Nico hates me for it. You might resent me."

I draw slow swirly designs in the hair at the back of his

head. "Then you'll have to work on that, won't you. Admitting you have a problem is the first of many steps. Step one, done. Step two, run all overbearing nonsense through Orlando. I have a father and an older brother who have too much of a say over my life. I want a sexy man, not a prison warden."

My father had power of attorney for several years, but I don't mention that to Rome. I don't like to think of that period at all.

I swallow hard. "I don't need another brother. I need a boyfriend who trusts me to be an adult."

Rome takes my wisdom in stride, nodding to tell me he will work on it.

It's not everything, but it's enough to assure me that what we have is real, and worth holding onto.

So that's exactly what I do for the next twenty minutes. I hold onto Rome, floating in our affection at a safe distance from the rest of the world.

We meet at our beach every Wednesday for the next two months, tangled under our tree, keeping each other warm while the world turns cold around us.

22

BLOOD NINJA DISCO

COLETTE

Though I lived overseas for ten years, Declan and I talked on the phone every day, never missing a beat in each other's lives. Though I would never say aloud that I have a favorite brother, everyone accepts that it's him. Declan knows all my secrets—except for my reoccurring dates with Rome.

Which isn't something I will be telling him ever.

Rome gave me a bracelet last week at our beach. Though my brothers rarely pay attention to my jewelry, wearing my new bracelet in front of Declan is a scandal that makes my heart race.

Declan talks with his hands, even when he's driving, just like me. I learned most of my bad habits from him. "You know, I'm up for a promotion. Just found out this morning that I'm being considered for shift supervisor."

My eyes widen as I blow out a long whistle. "That's

awesome. I mean, smart move on their part. You're the best paramedic they've got."

Declan bats his hand in my direction. "You're only saying that because it's true."

Though he looks like Fintan—short brown hair with a slight wave to it, upward slope of his nose and a rounder chin, his affinity for smiling makes him look entirely more charming than Fintan could ever become.

Declan's phone rings, so he answers it, letting the caller's voice float into the car so we can both hear it. "Hey, Dad. I'm with Coco. What's up?"

"That works out well, actually." My father sounds surprised, and unused to talking on the phone if it's not work-related. "I was thinking about something. Now that Coco is back in Mayfield, maybe we should do, like, family things."

Declan and I go silent, staring at each other with raised brows.

I mean, Declan and I do family things all the time. We're going to a movie right now, just the two of us. But spending time with my father and Fintan?

I cannot picture it.

Declan is the more congenial of the two of us, so his tone is chipper, despite the distrust in his eyes. "Um, sure. What do you have in mind?"

The sheriff pauses, as if he isn't sure how to ask for the thing he called to say. "I was thinking the three of you could come over for dinner. We could do like, a family dinner. That's a thing, right?"

My upper lip quirks in revulsion. We don't spend time together. We don't talk about things.

What's his game?

I shake my head at Declan, letting him know that this is not a good idea.

Declan shoots me a wry look, as if I am the one being irrational. "Sure, Dad. Text me a few dates, and I'll see what works."

"Really?" Our father sounds shocked that Declan would agree to it, and honestly, so am I.

My scowl at my brother cannot be helped.

"Sure. Coco and I will be there. It's a nice idea, Dad."

I glare at Declan after he ends the call. "Did you not see me shaking my head? I know you did."

Declan tilts his chin in my direction. "He's trying. I think it's nice." After a few beats of silence, Declan speaks without looking at me. "Have you talked to Dad lately?"

"We've been sticking to our steady diet of not speaking unless we have to. He meets with the Valentinos at my salon, but the last few times he didn't even come in to say hello. Why?"

Declan shrugs evasively. "No reason. He's been weird lately."

"Weird how?"

Why am I asking? I'm not sure I truly care.

"He's been... I dunno. Nice."

I snort. "I'll believe it when I see it." I consider this and then shake my head. "Probably not even then."

We share a giggle.

Declan keeps his eyes on the road, waiting for traffic to clear before he turns.

I fiddle with the radio. "Any idea why the sheriff wants a family dinner?"

Declan's lips purse. "Nope."

"It feels like a trap. Like he's going to tell us something horrible."

Declan doesn't answer right away as he pulls into the movie theater and parks. "I really don't want to talk about the sheriff tonight. This is all about taking a break from the drama."

I grin at my brother. "I'm so glad we're doing this. I've been on my feet all day. I've been at the salon so much that I can't believe I almost missed the release of Blood Ninja Disco VII."

Declan clucks his tongue at my messed-up priorities. He scolds me as he runs his fingers through his short brown hair. "The entire franchise is counting on us to keep the Blood Ninja Disco movies coming. If we miss opening day, they might switch to making movies that matter."

I shake my head at the state of the world. "The nerve."

Once we enter the busy multiplex, Declan orders a beer while I get our standard tub of popcorn and chocolate-covered raisins. The posters stretch from floor to ceiling, bragging theirs is the best movie of the season.

Movie night is a nice distraction from the fact that Rome has gone absolutely silent for four days. Our date is in two days. For the entire two months we've been dating, he has called me every single night, except for this week.

I'm hoping I won't be driving three hours this Wednesday for nothing.

As if Rome can sense when I am thinking about him, my phone rings while Declan grabs our beer at the concession stand across the lobby.

"I was hoping I'd hear from you. I'm out with Declan." It's a gentle warning that my words will have to be limited.

"I did it," Rome declares. "I went four whole days without calling you. I didn't nag you about your Friday night date. And I certainly didn't almost call you forty times."

My smile cannot be helped as I cradle the phone between my chin and shoulder. "I'm proud of you. Thank you. I miss your voice, though. Can we talk every night? I like that you call me."

"Thank God. Yes. This is the worst. Being with you only once a week is hard. I'll bring along some capicola from the West End deli that you like."

"Will you also bring those tight swim shorts, even though it's too cold to swim? Because I really like those."

The smile is obvious in his tone, and I love the sound

of it. His happiness is addictive to me. "Shame. I threw them out this morning. I'm going to bring baggy pants and a hoodie to swim in instead. I know how sexy that is to a girl."

"I'm swooning as we speak. In that case, I'll be wearing a clown costume."

"Mm. I'm going to have some filthy dreams tonight."

My voice lowers. "Oh, baby. Do you want my squeaky red nose on or off? I know how dirty you are."

"Leave it on. I need it. I want it."

I laugh because I can't help it. He just gets me.

Rome sounds relaxed. I wonder if anyone else gets to appreciate this side of him. "I love the sound of your laugh, little cannoli."

"You'll be hearing it tomorrow night when you call me again."

I'm grateful Declan's beer line is long. I meander to the hallway and sit on a bench, glad I can enjoy my phone call amid movie posters hung on the walls. "Fill me in on everything I missed this week."

The pause that hits my ears is not reassuring. "Nothing important. It's work stuff."

"That's the thing about girlfriends. When we ask about your life, we're including work stuff. I don't want to only know the Wednesday version of you. I want every part. I really like you, Rome."

I realize that I am pushing our boundary. I understand

why he wouldn't want to divulge vampiric drama to me. I am the sheriff's daughter, and much of what Rome does isn't exactly legal. He doesn't have much of an option, though. The West End is riddled with drug addicts now. My father doesn't police that area as he should. He arrests the addicts for possession, but they are offered no rehab treatment, as the humans are granted. He doesn't do the legwork to get to the root of the problem.

Rome handles things as best he can while my father looks the other way. They've both told me things are changing, now that they have their biweekly meetings, but I'll believe it when the evening news doesn't show that the vampire arrests for possession far outnumber the human arrests in Mayfield.

It's a broken system because my father broke it. The repair is messy and takes both sides humbly and diligently working together.

It seems Rome is sprinting toward a better future while my father is crawling.

Rome sighs. "You really want to hear it? This is how this sort of thing works?"

I grimace. "Honestly, I have no idea. I just don't want us to have a relationship where you feel you have to keep yourself from me. You don't have to tell me any of it. You might want to, though, and I'm happy to listen."

Another bout of silence greets me. I'm fairly certain he's going to change the subject, but I am pleasantly surprised when Rome opens up. "I don't want to half-ass our relationship. I want to show up for us."

My heart clenches with... it can't be love. It's way too soon for that. "I'm here."

For however long it takes Declan to get us our beer, I'm here.

Rome takes a long breath and then begins the novice practice of opening up. "I rely on my gut to tell me when something's not right, and my gut is acting up. There's a business on my end of the city that looks above board. My men have been doing what we can to kill the making and selling of halluci-blend in Mayfield, but it's still circulating."

Though I am pretty sure I understand the scope of things, I ask a question to clarify. "And this stuff is worse than the halluci-mend the Valentino family cooks up?"

"It's night and day different. I don't care if people do recreational drugs. That's their choice and sometimes it's the only medicine available to us. But this new stuff is deadly and hyper addictive. Someone messed with our original recipe. This bastardized drug is killing off vampires. I need to get to the root of the problem. I have to figure out how and who is putting halluci-blend only in the West End. Vampires are being targeted. I need to know who is behind it. I'm not sure I'm there yet, but I know something's fishy with Martin's Dry Cleaners."

"What does Orlando say?" I don't have enough information yet, but Orlando seems to always see and hear everything.

"We've been over their books enough times to go cross-eyed, and everything looks good. Orlando thinks my gut is broken."

I want to solve the problem, but listening isn't always about fixing. "Sounds like you're frustrated."

Rome exhales. "I am. The problem isn't going away. I know I'm right; I just have no proof."

"Maybe the sheriff can help you. Maybe you can push him harder to do some investigating, so it's not just you." I cringe, knowing I am stepping into fixing land, which isn't the point of listening. "I shouldn't have said that. It's your business, not his." I shouldn't be trying to push Rome and my father together. There's no reason for it. They are civil and mildly helpful to each other, which is as good as it's ever going to get.

I should be grateful. I'm sure I am.

But they can both do better.

"I don't know, tré-sur. I know he's your dad, and I respect him well enough to meet with him twice a month. But at the end of the day, he's still also the bastard who turned his back on us. He knows the West End has problems and he doesn't care. The vampires are citizens of Mayfield. I shouldn't have to ask him to do his job. He's turning a blind eye because he's racist, plain and simple. Asking nicely doesn't go all that far to undo rot like that."

I don't argue because no part of Rome's verdict is false. "You're right. I shouldn't have suggested it."

"Hey, it's a fine suggestion. Just not one I'm ready to pursue right now. Maybe someday."

"I'm sorry, Rome."

"Coletta," he scolds me in his loving way, "you didn't do anything wrong."

"Then I'm sorry my father's an ass."

He chuckles. "That, he is. I get it, though. He wants me to clean up after my people. I'm working on it. He's stepped back on overpolicing the West End. That was one headache."

I shake my head. "It still is. He hasn't stepped back enough. And he hasn't replaced the overpolicing with detective work that could actually do some good." I brush my thumb over each of my fingers. "It's okay to put a little pressure on him to speed up his progress." I stroke the diamond tennis bracelet Rome gave me, noting how effortlessly it sparkles.

"I can only change me. Elias is who he is." Rome's voice turns stern. "Listen to me, Coletta. Everything is fine. Understood? Your dad and I get along better than our families have in a decade. But we're still in the shallow end. I don't want you worrying that there's a problem. I'm respectful to your father."

Emotion clutches me around the throat. My father isn't worthy of respect. He was a key part in turning the public against the vampires after he and Daddy Valentino had their falling out. Rome asking my father to undo the damage he's done isn't too much to ask, nor is it disrespectful.

But Rome thinks I hold my father in high regard, so he's making sure I know he is being good to a racist old man on my behalf.

I couldn't adore Rome more if I tried.

I want to tell Rome exactly that, but when I open my mouth, the wrong words spill out. "Rome, I love you."

Rome fumbles on his end, his voice higher pitched than usual. "What?"

I cringe, then indulge in a steady stream of cussing. "Nothing! I didn't mean it. I take it back."

Or, at least, I didn't mean to say it out loud.

I don't know how to fix this, so I end the call with no explanation and no parting greeting. If I could burn my phone to undo my flub, I would.

I just ruined everything.

THE VIXEN AND THE BALLERINA
COLETTE

*W*hat did I just do?

I scared Rome. I know I did.

I don't want a conversation about this. I don't want to have said 'I love you' to him in the first place. I scrunch my eyes shut and slap my phone to my forehead before tucking it in my purse to distance myself from my crime.

I ignore the vibration of my phone. There's no way I'm answering that.

I catch Declan coming toward me with two tall cups in his hands.

I'm sure I radiate enough guilt to be palpable for miles. I offer my brother a cheery grin that I'm betting looks suspicious. "Hey, Declan. Which one's mine?"

"The one I didn't drink half of on the way here." He hands me my cup when I stand. Thankfully, the dim hallway casts a shadow on my nerves. I don't like keeping secrets from Declan, but this isn't one he would want to know.

Besides, it's movie night, not high drama day.

The Blood Ninja Disco movies are our absolute favorite, standing out among stupid movies and proving themselves the perfect spectacle of overbudgeted madness. Blood, plus ninjas, plus random choreographed dancing? You can't go wrong.

Or apparently, you can, as it's opening night for the show, and there are only a handful of people in the theater.

Declan and I are normal respectable movie patrons when we are with other people, but when it's the two of us, we are adorably obnoxious. We shout at the screen and eat way too much popcorn, throwing a few kernels when Sensei Travolta-San reveals his evil nature (which, by the way, I totally saw coming). We laugh too loud and cheer for our favorite characters to dance their cares away because in our deepest hearts, Declan and I are nine years old, begging the world for ninety minutes where we can stop pretending we are adults.

When the end credits roll, I've gone through just about every emotion one can experience, and am completely exhausted by the effort.

"I'm just going to say it." Declan holds both hands up toward the screen. "If this doesn't win an Academy Award, I'm going to lose faith in the entire system."

"Those award ceremonies don't appreciate the finer things."

We sit through the entire line of credits, not caring that there is only one other person left in the theater.

Rookies.

At the end of every Blood Ninja Disco movie, there's a choreographed dance number that should be everyone's anthem of greatness. Declan and I know the song—they do the same one at the end of every movie, but the choreography is new. My brother and I sing along at the top of our lungs, fully reveling in our juvenile moment, because that is who I never get to be.

When the movie ends and the lights come on, Declan and I make no move to stand, instead using the time to go over our favorite parts and reenact the fighting scenes with tremendous accuracy.

Declan is winded when I fake-kick his butt. "I missed this while you were away." He motions between him and me. "Us. Everyone else is so serious. It's all about the family drama. All about work. No one else appreciates good movies like you do."

I grin at my brother. Though he's five years older than I am, he is still the sibling closest in age. "I missed you, too, Declan. We won't miss any other releases together. Every time a new Blood Ninja Disco movie comes out, we're going together. None of this watching it in different continents and talking about it afterward."

"Agreed. No matter what else is going on in life, we need to have our priorities in order." He raises his hand to a high level above his head. "Blood Ninja Disco movies." Then he lowers his hand to his midsection. "Everything else."

"Deal."

There are still a few inches of popcorn left, so I grab up the tub and walk to the end of the aisle. Though there is no one else in the theater, I feel eyes on me.

That is the mark of a good Blood Ninja Disco movie.

Before we leave, I stop at the restroom, humming the closing credits song to myself as I wash my hands. When I push open the door to step into the main concession area, there is the usual bustle of people. Declan is still using the restroom, so I mill about, looking at posters and noting how they all pale in comparison to the Blood Ninja Disco advertisement, which of course, is 3-D.

Again, I feel eyes on me.

Instead of whipping my head around, I keep my eyes fixed on the poster in front of me, noting which direction I feel the heat coming from. I've always had a sixth sense about that sort of thing. Blame it on being my father's daughter.

Blame it on being my mother's daughter.

Blame it on me being the Last Deadblood.

I wait until I am certain the person staring at me is at

my four o'clock, then I turn with quick precision, locking my gaze where I know my Peeping Tom is located.

My mouth falls open as the beefy Valentino cousin does his best to fade between patrons.

Not so fast, Orlando.

My strides are quicker than his, even though his legs are longer. I've learned that if I roll my shoulders back, tilt my chin up and walk with purpose, people tend to clear out. The click of my stilettos warns anyone in my path to scatter because I am on a mission.

I catch up to Orlando quicker than I am sure he would like. I place my hand on his bicep to let him know the chase is over, and he lost. "Fancy meeting you here. Did you enjoy the movie, or was the sight of the back of my head more captivating?"

Orlando steels his reaction, scowling down at me and puffing out his chest to let his bulk do the heavy lifting of intimidating me. "It's part of the gig, Coco. I'm sure you know that. Rome doesn't date anyone without me vetting them first. If you two are going to pursue this terrible idea, I'm not going to stop you. But I am going to make sure you're not seeing someone else, and that you're not involved in anything that could hurt him."

I gape up at Orlando, my indignation fading in a breath. "You love him. That's why you're stalking me? You want to make sure Rome is okay?"

Orlando rolls his eyes at my casual use of the word

"love." "Of course. What other reason could there be? I certainly didn't waste fifteen dollars of my own money to sit through that stupid movie for my benefit."

I clutch my pearls, scandalized. "Just when I was starting to like you. That was the greatest piece of cinema ever made!"

Orlando is not convinced. "Whatever. Are we done here?"

"Almost."

Before he can brace himself, I throw my arms around Orlando, hugging him tight. His eyes bug, and he looks around wildly to make sure no one sees him being smothered with affection.

I don't care that he is the worst hugger in the world. I was always the only person who cuddled up to him, so I know he's out of practice. "I've missed you, Orlando. You're my big sweetie pie." Then I lean up and peck his cheek before releasing him. "If you need to keep tabs on me to make sure I'm not going to hurt Rome, I get that. Do you want my schedule for tomorrow?"

Orlando scrubs the part of his cheek that I kissed. "That's not how this works."

I boop his nose. "Yes, it is, because I say so. I'll be at my house tonight, and then at work in the morning until around seven. I'm not sure what my plans are for tomorrow. My father called, insisting we have a family dinner at some point. I swear, that's not a lie." My mouth pulls to the side. "You can't follow me there, because vampires aren't allowed to cross territory lines into the East End. Do you want me to call you when I get there?"

Orlando runs his palm over his face. "You are the worst."

I grin up at him, and then loop my arm through his like we're old friends (which we technically are). "When I'm at work, there's a coffee shop across the street. If you're camping out there to watch me, can you pick me up a decaf cinnamon vanilla latte? They are the absolute best."

Orlando shakes his head at me. "You have no sense of danger, do you. I'm the bad guy. You're the damsel."

I can't help my chuckle. "Are you sure? I thought I was the vixen, and you were the ballerina." I blow him a kiss. "But you'll always be my big sweetie pie. That is nonnegotiable."

"I always hated when you called me that." Orlando stares up at the ceiling as if praying for help from above. "Can this be over?"

"Oo! Do you want to go see Afterbirth Quake when it comes out next month? It looks so good. You can sit with Declan and me next time, instead of lurking alone in the back."

"I'm not sitting in a theater next to you."

I drop his arm and turn to face him, completely serious. "Why not? We were friends. Aren't we still?"

Orlando lowers his chin, refusing to meet my innocent gaze. "You're making this harder than it has to be."

I clasp my hands in front of me. "Should I be making it easier for you to not trust me?"

When he doesn't answer, my heart goes out to him.

I can feel the guilt radiating off his shoulders, so I reach out and thumb at his cheek, noting the prickle that might never go away. "It's okay, Orlando. Do what you need to do. I appreciate you caring if I'm good to Rome. It's a solid thing you're doing, looking out for him. He's a good man, and he needs someone like you looking over his shoulder to make sure no one stabs him in the back. I think if the two of us keep looking out for him, he might have a fighting chance to clear a path, so he can accomplish all the good he wants to for this city."

Orlando draws in a shaky breath. I know I've disarmed him. "Alright, Coco-bean. Run along." He motions toward the crowd. "Your brother is looking for you."

I reach out and squeeze Orlando's hand, my heart warming at his use of one of my many childhood nicknames. "It's going to be okay, Orlando."

He meets my eyes with a cloud of doubt. "You know that's not true. The two of you are doing more than playing with fire. You're on the cusp of starting a war. Pretend all you want, but that's exactly what's going to happen if your family finds out."

I want to laugh off Orlando's assessment, but he's spot

on. "If I could fall for any other man, I would. But Rome is it for me."

It's not until the words spill out of me that I realize they've been true for a while. I'm not sure if I am more relieved or scared, now that my exposed heart has hit the air.

Orlando bobs his head. "Be careful, alright?"

"Be safe," I echo, hoping that someday Orlando truly does have a better life than spending his evenings stalking me in his spare time.

I flit back into the crowd and flag down my brother, all the while feeling Orlando's eyes on me as we walk to the parking lot.

24

BAD BROTHER

COLETTE

*B*eing that Declan is my very best friend and my favorite brother, when he tells me he likes the shampoo from my salon, I see no reason not to make our stop my salon on the way home to gift him a bottle.

"It's just a better product," I tell him, only sort of bragging. "I know you think I'm saying that because I make it myself, but it's true. No fillers, no dyes, no sodium laurel phosphate."

Declan rolls his eyes as he turns onto the Midtown street where my business is located. "Thank God. I mean, that's the first thing I look at when I'm searching for shampoo."

I bristle. "It's the first thing you should be looking at. You could clean a car with that garbage. No, no. We have beautiful Kennedy curls. Best keep them from being polluted with sub-par ingredients."

He chuckles at me and runs his fingers through his shorter hair, pretending to be a supermodel. "Only the best for the best of the Kennedys."

I bump his fist with mine. "Hear, hear."

Declan frowns as he pulls into my parking lot, which, thanks to Rome, has flood lights installed. "Um, is there any reason why a Valentino would be here when your salon is closed?" He points to a car at the far end of the lot, which is the furthest point from the light. The car is only halfway shaded by the night, but I can see enough to recognize the black sedan with tinted windows.

I start to sweat, wondering why Rome would be here when I am not. "Let's not jump to conclusions," I warn my brother as he takes his gun from his hip holster. Anxiety spikes when I grasp at reasons why Rome might be here that would make sense to my brother.

I hate that my brother carries. I hate that I carry. I don't want to be in this much danger all the time. I don't want to expect that the violence of the past is always going to be coming for me.

"Stay here. I'll see what's going on."

It's my turn to roll my eyes. "As if I'd let you go in alone."

Declan sighs but doesn't argue with me more than that as he gets out of the car.

I reach down into my purse and pull out my pistol.

I also grab my phone and call Orlando.

Orlando's voice is gruff when he answers, but I cut to the purpose of my call to make the exchange short and semi-sweet. "Boy, could I use a stalker right about now. Is Rome inside my salon?"

"What? No. Why?"

"Because his car is in my parking lot afterhours and no one's in it. I'm pretty sure he broke into my salon." The night feels ominous now.

Orlando groans. "Nico borrowed Rome's car. Stay where you are. I'll handle it."

"I don't exactly have a choice. I'm with Declan. Get over here and handle your family."

"On it. Keep me in your pocket."

I mute Orlando's voice and drop my phone into the pocket of my pink pencil skirt as I grip my gun. I don't have my safety off. I have no intention of shooting a Valentino tonight. "Safety on," I chide Declan. "We are not shooting family."

Because that is exactly what the Valentinos used to be to us.

Declan's mouth tightens, but he complies, letting me call the shots. We stalk to the salon, entering through the backdoor.

A crash coming from the main waiting area tells me this is not a friendly visit from Rome, but possibly another hazing from Nico.

I can't believe I suspected it was Rome. Even with the evidence of his car in my lot, I should have had more faith in us.

What could Nico possibly be doing here? Is he ransacking my business again?

When Declan and I move further into the salon, I see a figure that is shorter than Rome, but any other dissimilarities are harder to pick out.

I harrumph, letting go of any attempts at sneaking when I flip on the lights. "Are you kidding me with this, Nico?"

Caught mid-vandalism, Nico freezes, but only for the briefest of moments. Then he pulls out his gun, aiming it directly at my head. "You shouldn't be here! All of this! You're done, do you hear me? Midtown doesn't need your business. We don't want your high and mighty help when nearly every other business in Midtown has signs up that read *Humans Only*."

Declan cocks his gun, which means the safety on his weapon is a thing of the past.

"No, Declan!" I shout, though I should be yelling at Nico.

I refuse to plead for my life. I made a promise to myself after my second abduction that I would never again beg for my life to be spared. I'll either die or I'll live. My words don't matter to a psychopath because we don't speak the same language. I can try reason. I can try logic. But I will never again beg.

Declan's forearms are taut, his words coming out of him in a growl. "Put the gun down, Nico. You take up your rage with the sheriff. This isn't how things are done."

I glance around at my business, grateful that we caught Nico before he did more than knock over my reception area. Money is spilled out on the floor and the monitor is most likely broken, but that's the worst of it.

Nico doesn't comply, keeping his aim trained on my face, which fights to compose itself. "This is how this is going to go. I'll leave now and no one will have to get hurt if you agree to close down this business and go. Not just go back to the East End, but leave Mayfield entirely. Move overseas again. Go back to Lonmure. That country loved having you. We're done with the chaos you bring."

My heart breaks right in front of him. "Why do you hate me?" I should be negotiating some sort of peace, but I am too sad to try.

Nico's rage comes out at a shout. "You killed my mother and my father!"

I fight to keep my voice level. "My blood killed them, yes. You hate my blood." I raise my hands in surrender. "So do I, so we're the same."

Nico's fist shakes. "We are nothing like the same! Do you hear me? We couldn't be more different. You walk around and people talk about your shoes, your hair and your bravery. I walk around and people gather their children away from me. You didn't ask to be born this way? Well, I didn't ask to be born this way!" He motions around my salon with his free hand. "Don't you see that you're stirring the pot? You're pretending change is possible, but look at nearly every other business in Midtown. They still have signs that say *Humans Only*. Your ideals mean nothing!"

I hate that he is right. The promise I made to myself that I wrote on a slip of paper burns against my breast.

Peace is Possible.

What was I thinking?

I move my hand over my heart. "I want things to change. I want the entire world to be our family vacations. Don't you see that? Can't you picture it?"

"No," Nico barks, his voice breaking. "We are different. Opening up a business and pretending the world is fixed is ignorant at best."

Declan inches toward me, his gun still aimed at Nico. "She isn't pretending anything, Nico. She's trying. She's standing up and marching to her own drum because the world needs a new song. Change isn't going to happen overnight. It may not happen in our lifetimes. But that doesn't mean she shouldn't try."

It's the loudest seal of approval anyone in my family has ever given me.

Nico snarls at Declan. "You're a medic who only treats humans. Fintan's restaurant is located in the East End, where vampires aren't allowed. This salon is a joke."

Declan straightens. "I'm a medic who has no training in treating vampires. You want to educate me, Nico? Be my guest. Put down the gun and teach me how to treat a vampire. I'll learn."

Nico scoffs. "Pass the blame to the establishment. How very human of you."

Declan's elbow touches mine. "You've got a problem with Fintan? Then wave a gun in his face. Don't pick on the only one of us who is taking a stand and doing the right thing. Colette isn't passing the blame. She's doing what she can. She's trying, Nico. You're destroying the only person who's making an effort."

Nico doesn't lower his gun. "I've got enough reasons to hate the person who got my parents killed. But I'm not pulling this trigger for them. I'm shooting because your dad left us with nothing. Rome wants this truce? Fine. I want a war. I want to settle the score and take from the sheriff the one person he loves. He did nothing when my mother was taken out. Nothing!"

At this, I laugh. Maybe I'm hysterical. Maybe I have finally snapped. "That's what this is? You want to ruin my business because you think my father cares about me? You want to put a bullet in my head because you think that will put a dent in the sheriff's stony heart?" I shake my head at my Nino-bear. "Oh, Nico. I thought you didn't believe in fairy tales." I spread my arms out to the sides, making myself a wider target. "Fire away, then. You'll see that the sheriff only cares about himself. I saw my father exactly zero times in the decade I lived overseas. He doesn't care about me in the least, and I think we both prefer it that way. You're right; he didn't protect all the citizens of Mayfield. The sheriff should have been serving the vampires, but he failed you." My laugh burbles out of me again, sounding just as unhinged as I feel. "Well, I've got news for you: he failed me, too."

Nico's lips purse. He looks confused at my insanity, though I can't believe it's taken me this long to crack. He holds his gun steady, still aimed at my face. His eyes narrow as his mouth twists in confusion. "No, you're daddy's little girl. It would break him if he lost you."

"You want to know where my father was on my sixteenth birthday?"

Declan grimaces, though his gun is still trained on Nico. "Don't do this, Coco. It's in the past. Don't dig it all up for Nico."

I laugh so hard that I bend at the waist, my hands on my knees. "I don't know! I don't know where he was! Isn't that funny?"

Nico studies my hysteria but doesn't say anything.

"You want to know where he was on my seventeenth birthday?" I am laughing so hard, I'm crying.

I've never cried about that.

I guess I was waiting to be held at gunpoint for emotions to come about—however fractured.

"I don't know!" I answer my own question. "How about my eighteenth? I'll give you one guess... Your guess is as good as mine, because I don't know! How about my nineteenth birthday? I'll save you the trouble. I don't know where my father was!" I am laughing so hard, I'm wheezing as tears stream down my face.

The second Nino-bear lowers his weapon, Declan gathers me into his arms, shoving his gun back in its holster. "Enough. Dad doesn't matter. Who called you on your birthday every year? I did. You know why? Because *you* matter. We don't care what he says, understood? Because we have each other." He squeezes me tighter. "He will never approve of anything we do. Even if we did everything by the book. It's his way. So we listen to ourselves, okay? Tap into what is true, not what we wish was true."

I laugh while crying on my brother's shoulder. Even as Orlando barrels in through the backdoor, we hold tight to each other.

Orlando's booming voice echoes through the salon, but I can't focus on his words. He is handling Nico, and Declan is handling my madness, which hasn't crested yet.

Orlando speaks with barely controlled rage to Declan over my shoulder while I laugh and cry with no end in sight.

My feelings don't matter about this entire topic, so I try my best never to let them near my psyche. I want to push out anything that might make me vulnerable, that might break me beyond what I can put back together myself.

So in that case, yes, I guess I am daddy's little girl.

25

COMING AND GOING
COLETTE

After sleeping at Declan's last night, I have a slightly healthier perspective on my morning. Though the sun isn't up yet, I am, and I'm ready to go fix my salon.

I'm hoping I won't find more damage than the knocked over reception station and cracked monitor, but you never know.

When I pull into the parking lot, Rome's car is still in the lot. I summon all my bravery, in case Nico is still here. But when I walk inside, I am grateful to find Rome by himself.

He is clad in his usual black slacks and fitted white dress shirt, complete with silver belt buckle and nice shoes. His dark, wavy hair is perfection, but for a little ruffling in the back that tells me he hasn't been to bed yet.

His expression when he stares at me is unreadable. He

doesn't look angry, sad or elated, but rather a mixture of all those things. "Colette."

"Aren't you the speedy cleaner. I came in early to get a jump on things, but I see you beat me to it." I glance at the reception station, noting that it looks tidier than it did earlier this week. "You got a new monitor, too. Thank you."

Rome's jaw is stern as he takes in the scope of me while clutching the broom. "Don't thank me. Be angry at me."

I tilt my head to the side, setting my purse on the nearest counter. "I think I'll save my anger for Nico." I motion to the salon. "You don't have to clean this up, you know. Nico made the mess."

"Yes, but I answer for the family. I didn't have Nico under control, so this happened. This is my fault." He leans the broom against the wall and then faces me, his hands tucked behind his back, chest puffed like a man facing a firing squad.

I gnaw on my lower lip, unsure how to handle this situation. "Rome, that's your hang-up, not mine. I don't see things that way, but feel free to punish Nico all you like." My shoulders sag. "He's miserable. However well you think he's doing, dial it back a whole heck of a lot. He's in pain, Rome."

"Well, he is now. I've seen to that."

I don't argue the Valentino's way of dealing with insurrection among their own ranks, but it certainly brings me no joy.

I study the bags under Rome's eyes and motion for him to join me on the couch in the waiting area as I sit. It's so brazen, sitting in open with him like this, but the shades are still down on the glass windows and door, so it gets to be our little secret.

Rome leaves a healthy amount of space between us, for which I don't blame him. I don't know which is worse: that I told him I love him two months in, or that his brother held me at gunpoint.

The love stuff. That's worse for sure.

"I need to end things between us right now," Rome tells me, ripping my heart out in a single sentence. He runs his hand over his tired face. "It's beyond complicated."

My hammering heart aches in my chest. I feel cold all over, inside and out. Nothing feels real. His words sink into my ears and mush into a ball of nonsense.

My heart feels hollow—empty and carved out. I made a spot for him, but he doesn't want it.

Devastation weights my bones as the shockwaves echo over my body.

I didn't see this coming, though maybe I should have. Neither of us are meant for relationships, even if it was with someone the world would approve of. We pushed the rules too far, leaping over them as if they weren't there for a reason.

I need a partner who can stand beside me. Even if he wasn't a vampire and we only had to deal with the complication that I am the Last Deadblood, it would require a man be stronger and more steadfast than most.

If Rome is not that man, I guess it's good I know now.

I point toward the back of the salon to stop myself from giving in to my urge to beg or argue. "The door is that way. If you want out, no one's going to stop you."

Except that I want to stop him. I want him to stay, even when it's hard—even though it might always be hard because I am who I am and he is who he is.

Rome leans forward, his elbows resting on his knees. "I need to end things, but I can't. Even though I know it's the better choice, no part of me can walk away from us." He turns his chin toward me, taking in my poorly composed confusion.

"You need to work on your communication skills, Rome. Are you breaking up with me or telling me that you're never going to break up with me?"

"I'm not sure," he replies honestly. Then he shakes his head. "I'm not breaking up with you, though I know that's the right thing to do. But I guess at the end of the day, I'm selfish, and I want what I want. I want to be with you, Coletta, even when betting on us is a poor gamble."

I tug on my fingers while I process his words. "Then let's take it slower."

Rome snorts. "Slower than this? I only get to see you once a week."

"Slow enough that you don't throw it all away because it's too hard."

Please don't throw me away.

"I'm going to ruin your life." Rome motions around the salon. "Nico is a drop in the bucket. If anyone found out about us? It would be a statement the world isn't ready to hear."

"Nobody ever wants to hear what I have to say, so that's nothing new. But I get it, Rome. I'm more than fine with keeping things secret. I thought I made that clear. It's as much for your protection as it is mine."

Rome lowers his chin. "I need you to forgive me."

I take in a long breath. "I already told you, there's nothing to forgive. You didn't trash my salon. Nico did. And I forgive Nico. I always have. Always will."

His hands tighten into fists and then release. "Not for that. Or not just for that. I need you to forgive me for staying. It's selfish, and I know it. Orlando set me straight a few hours ago. I told him I would end things because you deserve better. You should be able to go out with a man who can actually take you out. You should be able to be with a human. Someone with less blood on their hands."

I brush off his words, though they hurt me all the same. "What's the fun in that?"

He narrows one eye at me. "Don't do that. Don't be glib. Not when I'm trying to do the right thing."

"And the right thing is to make us both miserable?" I sit

up straighter on the couch. "Stay or go, but don't do either unless it's what you want."

He meets my gaze with genuine worry shining through. "You deserve better than me."

I turn to him and grip his collar, bringing him close because if this is our last moment together, I want to remember the smell of his cinnamon breath. "Actually, I'm the kind of girl who deserves to have whatever I want, and I want you."

Rome exhales, and in the next breath, his lips descend on mine to replace the foul words that tried to break us up. "I'm sorry. You're right." He deepens the kiss, pulling me onto his lap so he can run his hand over my thigh. "I'm in. I'm all in."

"Let's be selfish, Rome. Let's be selfish just this once."

Rome moans into my mouth, his tongue twisting with mine.

I love the taste of him even more than I am allured by the scandal of all we are and all we can never be. I want more.

So I take it.

Rome's mouth is ripe for the plundering. The rest of him might belong to Mayfield, but his lips are mine alone. They are soft yet firm, commanding yet letting me take when my need grows too great to tame.

Rome's fingers trill up my thigh. "I was stupid to think I could end this. Let the world come for us. I don't care." He kisses me again, his forehead pressed to mine while we let our hearts find the same rhythm, so we are not so alone in this world.

Rome kisses me for the next half hour, christening the couch until we are both breathless and bereft of reason. No matter how it all implodes, I will never bring myself to regret taking this chance.

"You. I want to be with you, Coletta."

"Only you, Rome. Only you."

And I know that my promise is true. Whether he stays or goes, I cannot fathom my heart without him tucked inside. For me, there will always only be him.

Even if the world hates us.

Even if they come for us...

...which they most certainly will.

I hold Rome close, trusting the thrum of my heart, even if it is determined to lead me down a path from which I can never return.

I can't go back. Not after this.

So I kiss him again, hoping the world doesn't tear us apart.

Love the book?

Leave a review!

26

THE BROKEN CITY

ENJOY A FREE PREVIEW OF "THE BROKEN CITY", BOOK TWO IN THE LAST DEADBLOOD SERIES

The Vampire and the Deadblood

It's hard to keep my nerves at bay when Rome and my father have their scheduled meetings. Though our relationship is new and predictably rocky, we have struck a deal. Rome agreed not to bring up my embarrassing "I love you" slip I made a few days ago on the phone while I was at the movie theater, and I agreed not to mention him almost breaking up with me because things are most certainly going to be complicated going forward.

It's going as well as one might expect the very first vampire-human pairing in history to unfold.

If anyone found out that the head of the Valentino

family was calling me—the Last Deadblood—every night, they wouldn't believe it.

Of course, no one would believe Rome has a poetic soul in the first place. They assume just because he inherited the mess of the West End from his father, that he doesn't appreciate the finer things.

But the man makes me raspberry cannoli from scratch. He reads me poetry on the phone at night.

He kisses like a filthy, filthy dream.

We have fallen into our rhythm of clandestine phone calls and precious flirts, as well as a once-a-week Wednesday date. Though I wish we could have a normal relationship, I've always known that was not in the cards for me, no matter which man is at my side. Frankly, I'm surprised I haven't received any threats from the revolution, claiming they will abduct me if I don't give them my blood voluntarily.

Of course they want my blood; it's the one thing that can kill vampires without fail. People fear what they don't understand.

They certainly don't understand Rome, or the entire race of people who were given a raw deal. The vampires are too beaten down to demand better.

Or perhaps the humans have stopped listening.

That's what these meetings between my father and Rome are supposed to be. The sheriff is supposed to listen and be helpful (imagine that), while Rome makes an attempt at trust.

It's a stretch for them both, but it happens twice a month outside my salon, and I love it every time. I want people to walk by my salon and see progress. I want them to see my sign that reads *Vampires and Humans Welcome* and feel a sense of peace about the world.

I really wish other businesses would follow suit. Midtown is a neutral space between the East and West sides of Mayfield. Still, my salon is one of the very few businesses that will actually cater to both races.

One step at a time, even if that step is tiny and feels like it is getting us nowhere.

The salon is busy, which makes me happy. But when the two show up for their biweekly chat, it's like a cloud comes over the lighthearted atmosphere. People inch away from the window but keep their eyes on the two heads of the rival families who used to be close.

Instead of lighting up like a giant Christmas tree at the sight of Rome entering my salon, I let Rachel greet him because she is tending to the front desk for this hour. Rome hands her a sealed envelope and tells her it's for the owner without meeting my eyes. Usually it's an effort to pretend I am uncomfortable with him in my business, but not such an effort today, given that he tried to break up with me the last time I saw him.

Rome is stunning, even from a distance. His obsidian hair highlights the brightness of his ice blue eyes. His angular jaw is strong and casts emotion so well that he rarely has need for a smile. He is tall and leonine, with broad shoulders and a trim waist. I never cared much about the uniform the Valentino men all wear—white dress shirt with the sleeves rolled, black fitted trousers and a silver belt buckle—but on Rome, it is perfection.

Then my father enters a minute later.

Now I'm sweating.

The sheriff doesn't know I am dating a vampire. *He couldn't possibly*, I tell myself. *I'm being perfectly normal.*

My father and I exchange a few words to convince each other that we have absolutely no bad blood between us, which is a constant dance we do. We don't talk about the fact that he sent me away when I was sick. We don't talk about him letting us all down by alienating the West End and doing a bad job at law enforcement for so long. Because of his bigoted negligence, there is precious little hope we will be able to dig Mayfield out of the hole in which it is mired.

No, we don't talk about any of it. I'm a good daughter.

Mostly.

"I'll be out there with the Valentinos. You still okay with us meeting here?" my father asks, his chin lowered as if he actually cares about my response.

His hair is thinner these days, his skin dry and sagging. Even his thick neck is wrinkled. Though he is only in his sixties, he looks far more weathered. I'm not sure if it's the job or if something deeper is going on. If not for his dismissive attitude toward the things that matter, I might think him an older relative of the man who sent me away when I was only fifteen. That man was scary to argue with. This man—the aged one standing before me—still inspires fear in my soul, but there is a weariness to him that makes me think new ideas might actually have a fighting chance.

I wave my hand to dismiss his words. "It's fine. Don't shoot up the place when you two bulls disagree over which one of you knits the prettiest tea cozy."

The sheriff snorts an airy laugh at my quip before exiting.

Huh. My father hasn't been coming in to greet me before his meetings with Rome. He did once when I cut his hair, but never since. We do a pleasant "you don't exist if I don't look at you" sort of dance, which has served us both well.

My steps are measured as I retrieve the sealed envelope from my mailbox slot and slip into my office. My door locks and I rush to my desk, tearing open the envelope to find...

What am I looking at? Ledger sheets?

A small note from Rome slips out. "I know Martin's Dry Cleaners is involved in the drug game that's killing the West End. Stayed up late trying to find the hole in their books. Stayed up later thinking of you. Maybe you can be my second pair of eyes."

A girlish smile takes over my features as an exhale rocks my body. He's not going to call me out on my embarrassing "I love you" slip, nor is he breaking up with me in a letter.

Thank goodness. We can pretend neither of those things ever happened.

Memories of our most recent dip in the lake flood my mind, bringing my gaze to my wrist.

The white gold diamond bracelet is far too dressy for work, but I can't help myself. He clasped it around my wrist the last time we went to our beach. I was in cutoffs and a sweatshirt, my hood on to fend off the brunt of the chilly autumn weather. We'd been laughing together and making out under our favorite tree when he fixed it on my wrist.

We get one date a week, and we spend it on a stretch of beach no one frequents this time of year. We wanted to be so far away that no one from Mayfield would see us.

When I gaped at the luxury, he held up a hand to stave off my spluttering. "For the record, this is me holding myself back. I put back the necklace I wanted to buy you last week, and I walked away from the bulletproof windows I wanted your car outfitted with two weeks ago."

I'd stared at the bracelet, much like I am doing now, wondering how my life took such a dramatic turn. Rome's affection is lavish and loud, even when we have to be silent about it.

Rome is a constant puzzle. He is committed to us completely, but whenever he realizes the danger to me that might come because of our relationship, he gets this altruistic streak that tells him to break things off for my safety.

I do my best to enjoy our relationship while it's here. While the world will still leave us alone.

Though I have an appointment in ten minutes, I comb over the copy of the ledger from Martin's Dry Cleaners. At first glance, things appear in order, but I know better than to brush off Rome's gut. If he thinks this business has something to do with the dreaded and highly addictive halluci-blend coming into Mayfield, then this is the place to look.

Some of the products they are buying I am not educated on, so I look up every single one, making a note of each business they've bought from so I can investigate their dealings, too.

This is turning into a longer project than I had anticipated. The spreadsheet I am putting together on my laptop is practically groaning at the amount of data that might actually lead to nothing important.

When I am interrupted by a knock, I cringe at the time. I am five minutes late for my client, which is not acceptable.

Victor pops his head in with a smile. "I shampooed your one o'clock. You want me to cut her, too?" He adjusts the brunette bun atop his head.

There's not a drop of judgment or anything passive aggressive in his question. Victor is being a team player, which is a truly good feeling. I love that I have surrounded myself with such solid people.

However, I despise that I am the one for which they are picking up slack. That's not me. "I've got it. Thank you, Victor. Count on taking my tip from this one, okay? Sorry. I got caught up."

Victor high-fives me and then runs a finger over his eyebrows to straighten them. "Don't sweat it. I've got your back, Boss."

To make up for my tardiness, I am extra chatty and on the ball while I tend to my client. When the next one comes in after I finish up with her, I notice that Rome is still at the table with my father.

They are usually done by now.

Orlando stands behind his cousin like a sentry, silent but visible enough to enforce respect. I hate that my father needs the visual reminder to be a decent person.

Orlando looks much like Rome, only taller and with a more intimidating musculature.

Also, I've seen Rome smile, but Orlando doesn't bother with levity, as it doesn't get the job done.

Usually, their meetings don't last more than half an hour, but the two are glaring at each other with an intensity that twists my stomach.

I grumble at the two under my breath, even though I know they cannot hear me. "Nice attempt at peace, guys. I'm sure everyone in Mayfield is convinced."

I don't hold my father in the high esteem many girls do their fathers, but part of me does wish he could take a shine to Rome. I also don't care if my eldest brother, Fintan, gets along with Rome, but it would be nice. Fintan doesn't really like me all that much, so I can't expect him to like my boyfriend.

But if Declan—my favorite brother and closest friend in the world—lives his whole life hating my secret boyfriend, that is going to be hard to swallow. One day, I will have to tell Declan. We don't keep secrets from each other. Not like this one.

My mouth goes dry as a horrible thought occurs to me.

I very much care if Rome is telling my father that we are dating.

He wouldn't do that. It's suicide.

My palms are sweating. My fingers start to twitch, so as soon as I finish the cut I am working on, I quickly excuse myself to my office once more, digging through my purse for my pills.

I swallow one without the need for water to choke it down. I can't take chances today, or I'll have a flareup at work. Stress is a major contributor to setting off the condition I swore to my doctor up and down I had mastered.

I count to sixty, knowing the fast-acting stuff is well on its way to helping me regain control before I lose myself completely.

Cutting hair with trembling hands is a bad idea. My condition leaves no room for my pride or trying to muscle through.

I place the flat of my hands atop my desk, breathing in and out slowly to make sure no part of me is shaking.

This is *my* business. *My* salon. I don't need to feel anxious here.

When I walk back into the bustle of my business, I notice the two bulldogs outside at the table have traded up from glares to a full-on argument. My father is talking wildly with his hands while Rome is sitting back in his seat, adding a word here and there with a curled upper lip.

The people sitting on my white leather couches in the waiting area aren't reading their magazines or looking at their phones. They are staring out the picture window at the burgeoning feud framed perfectly before them in front of my business.

My stylists are more intent on their work than ever before, only they're all silent, pretending they don't see the storm brewing outside.

This is not the atmosphere I set out to create. I have lavender walls, for crying out loud. That color bespeaks civility, not angry men gunning for each other.

I am wearing a short, teal high-waisted pencil skirt with a fitted baby blue blouse tucked into it. My hair has been woven into two French braids that twist into a chocolate-brown bun at the base of my neck.

I clearly dressed for a fun, peaceful environment.

I did not get out of bed today to referee their fighting.

I am an adult. I don't have to tolerate my father's tantrums anymore. I can stand up to him. I can make my voice matter.

"Be right back," I sing to Rachel and Victor, who stiffen and cast me warning looks to be careful.

Nah. Careful gets you nowhere.

I roll my shoulders back, draw myself up and stalk outside. I pull strength from the click of my heels. The formidable sound lets people know that a reckoning is coming.

"You think I have the resources to deal with your mess?" my father booms.

"Good afternoon, Miss Kennedy," Rome greets me, ignoring my father's temper.

How it's not clear that I am infatuated with this man, I'm not sure.

Rome meets my gaze and I wet my lower lip on instinct.

Not now, dummy.

I pull over a third chair to join the two heads at the table—something not even Orlando has the gall to do. I cross my left leg over my right and drum my fingertips on the lavender-painted table. "Good afternoon, Rome. Sheriff. Seems we have a bit of a problem, here. I've got it in my silly little head that I'm running a business, but you two seem to think that this salon exists solely for you to yell at each other. Care to share with the teacher what it is we're shouting about?"

My father doesn't like my condescending sing-song tone, which is exactly why I'm using it. He combs his fingers through his thinning light brown curls. Then he sniffs and swipes at his bulbous nose. "None of your business."

I force a throaty laugh. "Actually, it's none of *their* business." I point to my customers inside the building. "But this whole place is *my* business. *All* my business. So you're going to tell me what's going on, and you're going to do it with a smile. The peace treaty is only as solid as the smiles on your faces, so sell it better than this." My grin has a maniacal gleam to it as I lock eyes on my father. "Come on, now. Smile for the cameras. Everyone is watching us."

My father flinches because those are the exact words he used to say to me every time we went out in public when I was a little girl.

No, I am not about to make this easy for him.

Read *The Broken City* today!

ABOUT THE AUTHOR

USA Today bestselling author Mary E. Twomey lives in Michigan with her three adorable children. She enjoys reading, writing, vegetarian cooking, and telling her children fantastic stories about wombats.

While she loves writing fantasy, dystopian, and paranormal tales for her readers, Mary also writes romance under the name Tuesday Embers, and cozy mysteries under the name Molly Maple.

Visit her online at www.maryetwomey.com, and sign up for her newsletter, so you never miss a new release.